PROPHECIES

Signs of the Times, Second Coming, Millennium

OTHER BOOKS AND AUDIO BOOKS
BY MATTHEW B. BROWN:

RECEIVING GIFTS OF THE SPIRIT

JOSEPH SMITH
The Man, the Mission, the Message

SYMBOLS IN STONE
Symbolism on the Early Temples of the Restoration
(with Paul Thomas Smith)

THE GATE OF HEAVEN
Insights on the Doctrines and Symbols of the Temple

THE PLAN OF SALVATION
Doctrinal Notes and Commentary

PLATES OF GOLD
The Book of Mormon Comes Forth

PROPHECIES

Signs of the Times, Second Coming, Millennium

MATTHEW B. BROWN

Covenant Communications, Inc.

Cover image: *Five of Them Were Wise Virgins* by Walter Rane
Courtesy of the Museum of Church History and Art.

Published by Covenant Communications, Inc.
American Fork, Utah

Printed in Canada
First Printing: October 2006

11 10 09 08 07 06 10 9 8 7 6 5 4 3 2 1

ISBN 978-1-59811-222-1

CONTENTS

ABBREVIATIONS

PWJS—The Personal Writings of Joseph Smith
T&S—Times and Seasons
MS—Millennial Star
HC—History of the Church
JD—Journal of Discourses
CR—Conference Report
SSECB—The Strongest Strong's Exhaustive Concordance of the Bible
NWAF—A New Witness for the Articles of Faith
SAF—A Study of the Articles of Faith
MA—Messenger and Advocate
WJS—The Words of Joseph Smith
MFP—Messages of the First Presidency of The Church of Jesus Christ of Latter-day Saints
ADEL—An American Dictionary of the English Language
CD—Collected Discourses
CHMR—Church History and Modern Revelation
WP—The Way to Perfection
IE—Improvement Era
MD—Mormon Doctrine
DNTC—Doctrinal New Testament Commentary
DS—Doctrines of Salvation
OSS—Opening the Seven Seals: The Visions of John the Revelator
VM—The Vitality of Mormonism
AGQ—Answers to Gospel Questions
CHC—A Comprehensive History of The Church of Jesus Christ of Latter-day Saints
EMS—Evening and Morning Star
DWW—The Discourses of Wilford Woodruff

"This is a day of warning. It will be followed by a time of judgments. The Lord is about to shake terribly the kingdoms of this world. War, pestilence, famine, earthquake, whirlwind, and the devouring fire, with signs in the heavens and on the earth, will immediately precede the great consummation which is close at hand. These are the last days. All that has been foretold by the holy prophets concerning them is about to be literally fulfilled."

—Charles W. Penrose

INTRODUCTION

When the Prophet Joseph Smith looked above him in the wooded area directly adjacent to his family's home, on a now-famous morning in the spring of 1820, he viewed something that is rarely repeated and little understood: he saw a group of "many angels."[1] And standing before this great heavenly host was the Redeemer and Judge of mankind delivering a message that is seldom repeated even among Latter-day Saints. The Son of God declared on this profoundly significant occasion, "Mine anger is kindling against the inhabitants of the earth to visit them according to their ungodliness and to bring to pass that which hath been spoken by the mouth of the prophets and apostles. Behold and lo I come quickly, as it is written of me, in the cloud clothed in the glory of my Father."[2]

Here, at the inauguration of the dispensation of the fulness of times, was an announcement of the impending Second Advent of Jesus Christ being made by the Messiah Himself. Alongside the Savior's words spoken during the First Vision was a vivid visual representation of that very event—described in the Bible as follows: "For the Son of Man shall come in the glory of his Father with his angels" (Matt. 16:27).[3]

This focus on the prophecies of the last days was also notable during Joseph Smith's next encounter with a heavenly being. When the angel Moroni made his appearance in the fall of 1823, he informed Joseph that "the preparatory work for the second coming of the Messiah was speedily to commence; that the time was at hand for the gospel, in all its fullness, to be preached in power unto all nations, that a people might be prepared for the millennial reign."[4] The angel did not limit this message to a short announcement, however. To the young Prophet, he recited many passages of scripture that centered upon things which were to come to pass in the last days.[5] The angel also made Joseph aware "of great judgments which were coming upon the earth, with great desolations by famine, sword, and pestilence, and [he said] that these grievous judgments would come on the earth in this generation."[6]

Heavenly emphasis on prophecies of the latter days did not end with Moroni's visit. In the fall of 1828, Joseph Smith wrote a letter to his extended family "in which he declared that the sword of vengeance of the Almighty hung over this generation, and except they repented and obeyed the gospel, and turned from their wicked ways, humbling themselves before the Lord, it would fall upon the wicked, and sweep them from the earth as with the besom [or broom] of destruction" (cf. Isa. 14:23).[7] Furthermore, as the Savior relayed numerous revelations to the Saints through His authorized servant over time, He regularly referred to events that must come to pass in this day and also far into the future. In one of these revelations, the Lord laid a specific responsibility upon the Latter-day Saints. In Doctrine and Covenants 88, the Lord said to His modern disciples, "I give unto you a commandment that you shall teach one another . . . that you may be instructed more perfectly . . . in all things that pertain unto the kingdom of God" (v. 77–78). Included among those things that the Saints of the last days are commanded to study are "the judgments which are on the land," "the wars and the perplexities of the nations," and the "things which must shortly come to pass" (v. 77–79). As Elder John A. Widtsoe noted in relation to these verses, we are to study "the signs of the times, by which the observer may know that the day of the Lord is at hand."[8] The Latter-day Saints should not be like the rest of world by walking in darkness, said Elder Wilford

Woodruff. "They should have the light, and understand the signs of the times, and know the signs of the coming of the Son of Man."[9]

The great benefit gained by studying the prophecies of the last days is succinctly summarized by Elder Marion G. Romney. To the worldwide audience of the Saints assembled for general conference, he recited a sizable portion of Doctrine and Covenants 45, which notes in considerable detail the occurrences of the last days. He said to the gathered congregation:

> I hope we are all familiar with these words of the Lord and with His predictions concerning other coming events, such as the building of the New Jerusalem and the redemption of the old [Jerusalem], the return of Enoch's Zion, and Christ's millennial reign.
>
> Not only do I hope that we are familiar with these coming events; I hope also that we keep the vision of them continually before our minds. This I do because upon a knowledge of them, and an assurance of their reality and a witness that each of us may have part therein, rests the efficacy of Christ's admonition, "be not troubled."[10]

As a member of the First Presidency, Jedediah M. Grant once asked why it is that the Saints can be "perfectly calm and serene" during times when distress, turmoil, strife, pestilence, famine, and war erupt among the nations of the earth. His answer to his own question offers hope to agitated, apprehensive, and weary latter-day souls. He said that "it is because the spirit of prophecy [and the visions of the Almighty have] made known to us that such things would actually transpire upon the earth. We understand it, and view it in its true light."[11] Knowing what will happen in the future gives an individual a distinct advantage during troubled times. It is the hope of the author that this book will help readers to reach the stage where their hearts will not fail them during the turbulent days ahead (see D&C 88:91), because even though they might feel hemmed in by the darkness of the last days, they can know that a glorious light awaits them on the other side of the storm.

Notes to Introduction

1. Dean C. Jessee, ed., *The Personal Writings of Joseph Smith* (Salt Lake City: Deseret Book, 1984), 75–76; hereafter cited as *PWJS.* Unless otherwise noted, the quotations that are found throughout this book have been standardized to conform with modern spelling, punctuation, capitalization, and grammar.

2. Ibid., 6. This account of the words spoken by the Savior during the First Vision is written in the Prophet Joseph Smith's own hand. These words were recorded in 1832.

3. Jesus Christ states in a modern revelation, "And then they shall look for me, and, behold, I will come; and they shall see me in the clouds of heaven, clothed with power and great glory; with all the holy angels" (D&C 45:44).

4. *Times and Seasons,* vol. 3, no. 9, 1 March 1842, 707; hereafter cited as *T&S.*

5. A detailed look at the scriptures cited by the angel Moroni can be found in Appendix 1 of this book. See also Kent P. Jackson, "The Appearance of Moroni to Joseph Smith," in Robert L. Millet and Kent P. Jackson, ed., *Studies in Scripture, Volume 2: The Pearl of Great Price* (Salt Lake City: Randall Book, 1985), 339–66; Kent P. Jackson, "Moroni's Message to Joseph Smith," *Ensign,* August 1990, 13–16; Kent P. Jackson, "God's Work in the Last Days," in Kent P. Jackson, *From Apostasy to Restoration* (Salt Lake City: Deseret Book, 1996), 102–15.

6. *PWJS,* 204–5.

7. *Millennial Star,* vol. 27, no. 26, 1 July 1865, 407, hereafter cited as *MS.*

8. John A. Widtsoe, *Priesthood and Church Government,* rev. ed. (Salt Lake City: Deseret Book, 1954), 55. Joseph Smith admonishes the members of the restored Church of Jesus Christ with these words: "We shall . . . do well to discern the signs of the times as we pass along, that the day of the Lord may not 'overtake us as a thief in the night'" (Brigham H. Roberts, ed., *History of the Church*

[Salt Lake City: Deseret Book, 1948–1950], 3:331; hereafter cited as *HC.*). This viewpoint was echoed by Elder Bruce R. McConkie, who wrote, "Our obligation is to discern the signs of the times lest we, with the world, be taken unawares" (*The Millennial Messiah* [Salt Lake City: Deseret Book, 1982], 405).

9. George D. Watt, ed., *Journal of Discourses* (Liverpool, England: Samuel W. Richards and Sons, 1852–1886); 12:279, hereafter cited as *JD.*

10. Conference Report, Oct. 1966, 52; hereafter cited as CR.

11. *JD,* 2:147.

CHAPTER 1

SIGNS OF THE TIMES

Latter-day Saints have been informed in Doctrine and Covenants 45 that in the last days "signs and wonders . . . shall be shown forth in the heavens above, and in the earth beneath." These earthly and heavenly occurrences are specifically identified as "the signs of the coming of the Son of Man" and are thus to be considered in connection with the Second Coming of Jesus Christ (v. 39–40). The Lord has stated in modern revelation that members of His Church have the opportunity to "know the signs of the times, and the signs of the coming of the Son of Man" (D&C 68:11) and that they should, in fact, be "looking forth for the signs of [His] coming" (D&C 39:23).

Exodus 4 helps explain what the phrase "signs and wonders" means. In this chapter of the Old Testament, Jehovah sends Moses to speak with Pharaoh about the redemption of the Lord's people. Moses is directed to show forth certain signs to Pharaoh in order to encourage a cessation of Egypt's wicked behavior—the enslavement of the Israelites (v. 9, 17, 28, 30). The Hebrew word translated as "signs" in Exodus 4 is *ot*, which in one instance is defined as "a signal or event that communicates."[1] The Lord also speaks in the same section of scripture about Moses preparing to show "wonders before Pharaoh" (v. 21). The Hebrew word translated as "wonders" is *mopet*, and it can also be rendered as "miracles."[2] Equivalent Hebrew words are utilized in Daniel 6:26–27, where it is stated that "the living God . . . worketh signs and wonders in heaven and in earth." Thus the "signs and wonders" mentioned in Doctrine and Covenants 45 can be understood to be "signals and miracles."

One other detail mentioned in the episode with Moses can help to clarify revelations that speak of the signs of the times. In Exodus 4:8, the Lord refers to "the voice of the . . . sign." In this passage of ancient scripture, the Hebrew word translated as "voice" is *qol*, meaning, in one sense, "to cry out or proclaim."[3] Phraseology similar to that found in Exodus can be found in Doctrine and Covenants 88. There, the Lord, speaking to the Saints of the last days, says, "After your testimony [to the nations of the earth] cometh wrath and indignation upon the people. For after your testimony cometh the testimony of earthquakes. . . . And also cometh the testimony of the voice of thunderings, and the voice of lightnings, and the voice of tempests, and the voice of the waves of the sea heaving themselves beyond their bounds" (v. 88–90; emphasis added). An explanation of this type of language can be found in section 43 of the Doctrine and Covenants. In this section, the Lord makes it clear that after His servants have called upon the nations to repent in preparation for "the great day of the Lord," or the Second Coming, and their voice has been rejected, God will deliver the same message of repentance with much stronger force. He will call upon the inhabitants of the earth to repent by "the voice of thunderings, and by the voice of lightnings, and by the voice of tempests, and by the voice of earthquakes, and great hailstorms, and by the voice of famines and pestilences of every kind" (v. 20–25). Thus, some of the signs of the times, such as those just mentioned, should be considered a call to repentance, issued by the Lord Himself.

Signs of the times are manifested to forewarn mortals of the approach of the Second Coming so they have ample time to prepare accordingly. President Joseph F. Smith adds another dimension to heaven-sent signs, suggesting that "severe, natural calamities are visited upon men by the Lord for the good of His children, to quicken their devotion to others, and to bring out their better natures." However, he also states that "they are the heralds and tokens of His final judgment, and the schoolmasters to teach the people to prepare themselves by righteous living for the coming of the Savior."[4] As the Lord has said, when the people see the signs, "then they shall know that the hour [of the Second Coming] is nigh" (D&C 45:38). Proper preparation for the Second Coming is necessary, for the day of the Messiah's coming is described in scripture as being both "great" and "terrible" (Joel 2:31). It will be a day when the Lord will not spare any who "do wickedly" or, in other words, who "remain in Babylon." At that day such persons will "be as stubble" because the Lord will "burn them up" (D&C 64:24). The cry is to be sounded abroad: "Go ye out from Babylon. Be ye clean. . . . Go ye out from Babylon; gather ye out from among the nations. . . . Go ye out . . . from the midst of wickedness, which is spiritual Babylon" (D&C 133:5, 7, 14).

In scriptural texts, the Lord speaks of signs that occur on earth and those that take place in heaven. Knowledge of both types of signs assists the Saints in understanding the events of the last days and preparing for the Second Coming of the Son of God.

Signs on the Earth

Signs on the earth fall into two general categories: those connected with the righteous and those connected with the wicked. Of those associated with the righteous, some have already been fulfilled, some are in the process of fulfillment, and others are destined to come to pass in the future.

The Great Apostasy

The Great Apostasy is one of the signs of the times that has already been fulfilled but is also a condition still in progress. Elder Bruce R. McConkie said of this momentous event, "This is the first great sign of the times; out of it all others grow. It contains the seeds of evil from which the fruits of wickedness, despair, and doom are harvested. There is no hope for the world, except through the gospel of the Lord Jesus Christ; without it, all men remain carnal, sensual, and devilish by nature and are never reconciled to their God through the mediation of His Son."[5] The Great Apostasy placed men and women in this very undesirable set of circumstances, and they remain there until their reconciliation is effected through their personal righteousness and obedience to the authentic plan of salvation.

In the Joseph Smith Translation of 2 Thessalonians 2, the first Prophet of the last dispensation reveals that in New Testament times it was understood that "the day of Christ" or the "coming of our Lord" would not take place until there was a "falling away first." This passage of scripture repeats the idea, in explicit terms, that Jesus Christ's "coming is not until after there cometh a falling away" (emphasis added). This was (and for most of the world, still is) a period wherein Satan—the son of perdition, the man of sin, the wicked one—asserted that he himself was God. This period of apostasy took place "by the working of Satan with all power, and signs and lying wonders." Second Thessalonians explains that the Savior will allow this "mystery of iniquity" to continue to work only "until the time is fulfilled that [Satan] shall be taken out of the way." Then "the Lord shall consume [the unrighteous] with the spirit of his mouth, and shall destroy [them] with the brightness of his coming" (v. 1–10).

Establishment of God's Kingdom

Perhaps the most important of all the signs connected with the last days is the establishment of the kingdom of God on the earth. The Lord has confirmed that He has "committed the keys of [His] kingdom [to the earth again], and a dispensation of the gospel for the last times" (D&C 27:13). Presiding Bishop LeGrand Richards taught a general conference audience an important lesson in regard to this subject:

> If the inhabitants of this earth had the ability and the power to read the signs of the times, they would know that already the Lord has given far more than the darkening of the sun or obscuring the light of the moon or causing the stars to fall from heaven, for what He has accomplished in the establishment of His kingdom in the earth in these latter days, and the unseen power operating in the world for the accomplishment of His purposes, are greater signs than any of these phenomena that we read about—the signs of His coming.[6]

Thus the spectacular and terrifying physical signs that are slated to be seen by the eyes of humanity pale in comparison to the corporeal presence of the Lord's kingdom and to the work that it is foreordained to be accomplished before the Master returns.

In the Old Testament, Daniel prophetically interprets a dream about a stone cut out of a mountain "without hands"—meaning that the stone was created by a divine agency, not one of mortal origin. The stone cut without hands destroyed the kingdoms of the world and grew ever larger until it became a mountain and filled the whole earth. Daniel saw and understood that in the future, a kingdom would be set up by the God of heaven which would never be destroyed (Dan. 2:31–45). Doctrine and Covenants 65 provides some insightful commentary on these Old Testament verses. This section of modern revelation teaches that the stone represents the restored "gospel" which is to "roll forth, until it has filled the whole earth." Latter-day Saints are given the directive to "call upon the Lord, that His kingdom may go forth upon the earth, that the inhabitants thereof may receive it, and be prepared for the days to come, in the which the Son of Man shall come down in heaven, clothed in the brightness of his glory, to meet the kingdom of God which is set up on the earth" (D&C 65:2, 5).

This is necessary so that God's "enemies may be subdued" and so that He may be glorified on earth as He is in heaven (v. 6).

Publication of Ancient Scripture

The publication of the Book of Mormon is another of the prophesied signs of the times that has already come to pass. When the Lord appeared to the Nephites in the New World after His Resurrection, He told them specifically that the coming forth of the writings in the Book of Mormon would be a "sign" that certain things were about to take place, such as: (1) preaching the fulness of the gospel among the Israelites, (2) gathering together the dispersed of the house of Israel, and (3) the establishment of Zion (see 3 Ne. 20:24–46; 21:1–7).

In the Book of Mormon's final collection of scriptural writings, Jesus Christ declares that another set of ancient scriptures is designed to serve as a sign to mankind. In Ether 4, the Lord states that the revelations which He caused to be recorded by the Apostle John were to be unfolded or brought forth before the eyes of all people. When this happened, the Lord said, then it would be known by members of the house of Israel that the work of God the Father had commenced upon all the face of the land, and also that the things written in the documents prepared by John were about to come to pass (v. 16–17).

The Appearance of Elijah

In Malachi 4, Jehovah utters a prophecy about the last days that is familiar to most Latter-day Saints. He foretells that "before the coming of the great and dreadful day of the Lord," He will send the prophet Elijah back to the earth to turn the hearts of fathers and children toward each other to prevent a divine curse from befalling the earth (v. 5–6). The angel Moroni repeated this prophecy to Joseph Smith on the night of September 22, 1823, but he quoted it somewhat differently: "Behold, I will reveal unto you the Priesthood, by the hand of Elijah the prophet, before the coming of the great and dreadful day of the Lord. And he shall plant in the hearts of the children the promises made to the fathers, and the hearts of the children shall turn to their fathers. If it were not so, the whole earth would be utterly wasted at His coming" (D&C 2:2–3).

The fulfillment of this prophecy, found in Doctrine and Covenants 110:13–16, is Joseph Smith and Oliver Cowdery's experience in the Kirtland Temple on April 3, 1836.

> After this vision had closed, another great and glorious vision burst upon us; for Elijah the prophet, who was taken to heaven without tasting death, stood before us, and said:
>
> "Behold, the time has fully come, which was spoken of by the mouth of Malachi—testifying that he [Elijah] should be sent, before the great and dreadful day of the Lord come—
>
> To turn the hearts of the fathers to the children, and the children to the fathers, lest the whole earth be smitten with a curse—
>
> Therefore, the keys of this dispensation are committed into your hands; and by this ye may know that the great and dreadful day of the Lord is near, even at the doors."

Commenting on Malachi's statement about Elijah, the Prophet Joseph Smith said that temple work for the dead will be the key to avoiding the ominous curse associated with the Second Coming. This sacred work will create a "welding link" between the fathers and children, even "a whole and complete and perfect union" (D&C 128:18). Thus it appears that the Lord requires His authorized representatives to put His kingdom in order on both sides of the veil before He comes to personally rule and reign over it for a thousand years. Blessed is the faithful and wise steward who keeps the order of his lord's household while he is away—taught the Master in the meridian of time (see Luke 12:42–43). In turn, cursed is the steward who neglects to properly prepare for the day of his lord's return (see Luke 12:44–47).

Gospel Preached in All the World

In the Joseph Smith Translation of the Bible, the Redeemer prophesies that the "gospel of the kingdom shall be preached in all the world, for a witness unto all nations, and then shall the end come, or the destruction of the wicked" (JST, Matt. 24:32; see also JST, Mark 13:36).

Elder Bruce R. McConkie has written, in regard to this prophecy, "The gospel is to go to every nation and kindred and tongue and people before the Lord returns. All peoples are to hear the warning voice so they can prepare for the coming of Him who will take vengeance upon the wicked and ungodly. This requisite has yet to be fulfilled," said Elder McConkie; "indeed, we have done little more than scratch the surface where our worldwide preaching commission is concerned. This labor cannot be accomplished in full until the Church is much bigger and stronger than it now is."[7]

It follows, as a natural consequence of the gospel being preached in all the world, that there will be Latter-day Saints located throughout the nations of the earth before the Lord descends the second time. The prophet Nephi was shown anciently that before the Second Coming the "dominions" of the Church of the Lamb will be small in comparison with the rest of the world, yet the Saints will be found "upon all the face of the earth" (2 Ne. 14:12–14).

The goal of sending the gospel out among the nations of the world is to gather the scattered remnants of Israel and any other individuals who will hearken to the voice of the Good Shepherd. In the words of Doctrine and Covenants 84, the Savior's Church has been specifically "established in the last days for the restoration of His people" and for "the gathering of His Saints" (v. 2). In conjunction with the work of gathering Israel, Jesus Christ has prophesied that "before the great day of the Lord shall come, Jacob [or Israel] shall flourish in the wilderness, and the Lamanites shall blossom as the rose" (D&C 49:24). The keys of authority for the expansive work of gathering were delivered by the prophet Moses in the Kirtland Temple on April 3, 1836. He gave to Joseph Smith and Oliver Cowdery on that occasion "the keys of the gathering of Israel from the four parts of the earth, and the leading of the ten tribes from the land of the north" (D&C 110:11). Elder James E. Talmage testifies that "the return of the tribes [of Israel] after their long and wide dispersion is made a preliminary work to the establishment of the predicted reign of righteousness with Christ upon the earth as Lord and King; and its accomplishment is given as a sure precursor of the millennium."[8]

Enjoyment of the Gifts of the Spirit

Enjoyment of spiritual gifts is another prophesied sign of the times in continual fulfillment. In the Old Testament, Joel 2 is replete with themes that are traditionally associated with the Second Coming. In verse 28, the Lord says, "I will pour out my [S]pirit upon all flesh; and your sons and your daughters shall prophesy, your old men shall dream dreams, your young men shall see visions." This prophecy from Joel's writings is repeated in the New Testament book of Acts, where it is made clear that the fulfillment of these things will "come to pass in the last days" (2:16–17).

Evidently, Joseph Smith first learned of the idea of spiritual gifts during the spring of 1820 when he went to pray in what is now known as the Sacred Grove. According to Orson Pratt, Charles W. Penrose, and Lorenzo Snow, the Father and the Son explained to Joseph the loss of these blessings through the process of apostasy and told the young Prophet of their impending reestablishment.[9] Three years after the First Vision, the Prophet Joseph Smith received a heavenly reminder regarding the restoration of spiritual gifts. When the angel Moroni visited Joseph in September 1823, he not only quoted Joel 2:28, but he also reportedly said, "*With signs and with wonders,* with gifts and with healings, with the manifestations of the power of God, and with the Holy Ghost, shall the hearts of the faithful be comforted" (emphasis added).[10]

Times of the Gentiles Fulfilled

The angel Moroni also brought another biblical prophecy from the Bible to the attention of Joseph Smith. He said, "The fulness of the Gentiles was soon to come in" (see Rom. 11:25).[11] In an expanded version of this conversation between angel and Prophet, Oliver Cowdery records that the heavenly messenger explained:

> In consequence of the transgression of the Jews at the [first] coming of the Lord, the Gentiles were called into the kingdom, and for this obedience, are to be favored with the gospel in its fullness first, in the last days; for it is written: "The first shall be last, and the last first." Therefore, when the fullness of the gospel, as was preached by the righteous, upon this land, shall come forth, it shall be declared to the Gentiles first, and whoso will repent shall be delivered, for they shall understand the plan of salvation and restoration for Israel, as the Lord manifested to the ancients. . . .
>
> Therefore, as the time draws near when the sun is to be darkened, the moon turn to blood, and the stars fall from heaven, the Lord will bring to the knowledge of His people His commandments and statutes, that they may be prepared to stand when the earth shall reel to and fro as a drunken man, earthquakes cause the nations to tremble, and the destroying angel goes forth to waste the inhabitants at noonday: for so great are to be the calamities

> which are to come upon the inhabitants of the earth, before the coming of the Son of Man the second time, that whoso is not prepared cannot abide; but such as are found faithful, and remain, shall be gathered with His people and caught up to meet the Lord in the cloud.[12]

During the "fulness of the Gentiles," the Gentile nations shall possess "the fulness of the gospel of the Messiah" and will have the responsibility of spreading it abroad to nations that have opened their doors for its reception. This era is presently under way. The "grafting in of the natural branches" of the house of Israel takes place through what is called "the fulness of the Gentiles . . . in the latter days" (1 Ne. 15:13). There will come a point when "the times of the Gentiles [will] be fulfilled" (D&C 45:30) and the gospel will be taken to the Jews, because the Lord has commanded, "Call upon all nations, first upon the Gentiles, and then upon the Jews" (D&C 133:8). The Joseph Smith Translation of Luke 21 describes the timeframe for the fulfillment of the Gentile era:

> In the generation in which the times of the Gentiles shall be fulfilled, there shall be signs in the sun, and in the moon, and in the stars; and upon the earth distress of nations with perplexity, like the sea and the waves roaring. The earth also shall be troubled, and the waters of the great deep;
>
> Men's hearts failing them for fear, and for looking after those things which are coming on the earth. For the powers of heaven shall be shaken.
>
> And then shall they see the Son of Man coming in a cloud, with power and great glory.
>
> And when these things begin to come to pass, then look up and lift up your heads, for the day of your redemption draweth nigh. (v. 25–28)

The Establishment of Zion

When the prophet Enoch conversed with the Lord about events that would occur on the earth, he learned that a holy city will be established called "New Jerusalem" and "Zion." This city will have a temple and will be a place where the Saints of the Most High will gather and "[look] forth for the time of [the Savior's] coming" (Moses 7:62–65). Modern-day revelation explains that New Jerusalem—located on the American continent—will be a place where the Lord's disciples can "prepare their hearts and be prepared in all things against the day when tribulation and desolation are sent forth upon the wicked" (D&C 29:8; 57:1–3; see also 3 Ne. 20:22; Ether 13:4–6, 8).

The preliminary steps for the establishment of the holy city of Zion have already taken place, inaugurated near the beginning of the dispensation of the fulness of times.[13] But New Jerusalem will not be the only major place of gathering for God's people in the last days. In speaking of the Second Coming, the Lord Himself has said,

> Yea, let the cry go forth among all people: Awake and arise and go forth to meet the Bridegroom; behold and lo, the Bridegroom cometh; go ye out to meet him. Prepare yourselves for the great day of the Lord. Watch, therefore, for ye know neither the day nor the hour. Let them, therefore, who are among the Gentiles flee unto Zion. And let them who be of Judah flee unto Jerusalem, unto the mountains of the Lord's house (D&C 133:10–13).

The Prophet Joseph Smith pronounced the timeframe for the fulfillment of these expectations when he said that "Zion and Jerusalem must both be built up before the coming of Christ. . . . When these cities are built then shall the coming of the Son of

Man be."[14] The Prophet expounded upon this idea when he referenced Ezekiel's Old Testament prophecies. He said that Judah must return to Old Jerusalem, the city and the temple must be rebuilt there, "water [must] come out from under the temple," and "the waters of the Dead Sea be healed. It will take some time to build the walls and the temple, and all this must be done before [the] Son of Man will make His appearance."[15] Elder Bruce R. McConkie explains who will be involved in the construction of the temples of the Old and New Jerusalems. He taught that "before the second coming, gathered Judah, as directed by Ephraim, shall build up anew the Old Jerusalem and prepare therein a holy temple; and gathered Ephraim, aided by Manasseh, shall build a New Jerusalem in an American Zion and prepare therein a holy temple. It is to these two temples in particular, that the Lord shall come at His glorious return, and it is from these two cities—Zion in America and Jerusalem in Old Canaan—that the governance and worship of the world will be directed."[16] In other words, those who have gathered into the restored Church of Jesus Christ will build the great temples of the Old and New Jerusalems.

Conditions Among the Wicked

The Master prophesied during His earthly ministry that, near the time of His Second Coming, "iniquity [would] abound" (JST, Matt. 24:31). In modern times He has declared the realization of this expectation, saying, "Darkness covereth the earth, and gross darkness the minds of the people, and all flesh has become corrupt before my face" (D&C 112:23).

In the New Testament, the Savior likened the era prior to His Second Coming to past periods of pervasive wickedness on the earth, referring specifically to the days of Noah and of Lot (see Luke 17:26–30; Matt. 24:37–39). The book of Moses includes details of the abounding wickedness in Noah's day, with the Lord decreeing destruction upon the inhabitants of the earth during that age—a day when "the power of Satan was upon all the face of the earth" (Moses 7:23–24), so much so that the planet was figuratively "veiled . . . with darkness" (Moses 7:26). According to Moses' historical account, the people of this time were prideful, thinking that they were "of great renown" (Moses 8:21). The people rejected the Lord's ordained ministers who tried to teach them the gospel and also discarded the idea that they would be destroyed if they did not repent (see Moses 8:19–20, 24). They were "without affection, and they hate[d] their own blood" or family members (Moses 7:33); they were "corrupt" in their hearts (Moses 8:29), and evil pervaded their thoughts continually (see Moses 8:22; 7:36). Not only did they engage in immoral conduct (see Moses 8:15), but they were "filled with violence" (Moses 8:28). So complete was their degradation that they even sought the murder of righteous individuals (see Moses 8:18).

In the days of Lot, the inhabitants of the cities of Sodom and Gomorrah exhibited similar sinful behavior and abominations shortly before "it rained fire and brimstone from heaven, and destroyed them all" (Luke 17:30). The prophets Ezekiel in the Old Testament and Jude in the New Testament list the iniquities of Sodom as (1) pride, (2) "fullness of bread" or luxuriant living, (3) abundant idleness, (4) failure to care for the poor and needy, (5) idolatry, (6) contempt for others, (7) fornication, and (8) "going after strange flesh" or homosexuality[17] (see Ezek. 16:49–50; Jude 1:7).

The prophet Moroni saw a vision of conditions that would prevail in society during the last days, a vision at once instructive and disturbing—but undeniably prophetic. In Mormon 8, Moroni records that many people will foster a sense of pride through the wearing of fine apparel. But pride is to reach out beyond the level of individuals and also infect people on the organizational level. Churches and their leaders will become prideful and defiled—offering forgiveness for money; neglecting the poor, the needy, the sick and afflicted; and seeking after the praise of the world. In addition, a false doctrine will spread claiming that no matter what a person does, God will uphold him at the last day or the day of judgment. Furthermore, it will be said during this time period that miracles are done away, and the power of God will be flatly denied. Moroni learned that this rotting of the soul will also manifest itself in more aggressive forms, such as envy, strife, malice, deceitfulness, robbery, persecutions, and whoredoms. Finally, he saw that the situation will deteriorate so badly that the innocent blood of the Saints will be shed through secret combinations and works of darkness (v. 26–41; cf. 2 Ne. 28:3–15).

Additional insight on the nature of errant society in latter times is present in the writings of the Apostle Paul. This stalwart man of God warned in 2 Timothy 3 that "in the last days perilous times shall come," then lists those activities and attitudes that will blacken the souls of the sinful. Individuals, he said, will become "lovers of their own selves, covetous, boasters, proud, blasphemers, disobedient to parents, unthankful, [and] unholy." They will be "without natural affection [or hard-hearted], trucebreakers, false accusers [or slanderers], incontinent [or without self-control], fierce [or violent], despisers of those that are good [or scorners]." Some will become "traitors," "heady [or rash], high-minded [or conceited], [and] lovers of pleasures more than lovers of God." They will be "led away with divers lusts," be "ever learning, and never able to come to the knowledge of the truth . . . [because they] resist the truth," and possess a form of godliness but deny its essential power. Having "corrupt minds," they will be reprobate [or rejecters] concerning the faith" of the gospel. They will be known as "seducers [or imposters];" they will go about "deceiving, and being deceived" (v. 1–8, 13).

The imposters referred to by Paul are also mentioned in Joseph Smith's inspired rendition of Matthew 24, where we read that "false prophets" and "false Christs" will arise in the world and show great signs and wonders to the earth's inhabitants. So convincing will be their charade that "if possible" they will deceive even members of the Lord's restored Church (JST, Matt. 24:23).

During the administration of Brigham Young, the First Presidency of the Church issued a general epistle that identified some of these imposters. The Presidency declared, "The increase of seers, and wizards, and diviners, and familiar spirits, and soothsayers, and astrologers, who are charming the nations with their magic arts, lulling the foolish to sleep with their magnetic influence, deceiving priests and people by their necromancy, calling rain, snow, and fire from heaven, and scattering abroad hoar frost like a winter's night. . . . All these signs, and . . . many more like things [are the fulfillment of prophecies that] should come to pass in this generation, as signs of the second coming of the Son of Man."[18]

Dallin H. Oaks of the Quorum of the Twelve Apostles attests to the fact that the long-predicted degradation of mankind has indeed taken place in modern times and become widespread. This downward spiral has sometimes been encouraged or allowed by people who logically should have attempted to prevent it. Elder Oaks reports:

> Evil that used to be localized and covered like a boil is now legalized and paraded like a banner. The most fundamental roots and bulwarks of civilization are questioned or attacked. Nations disavow their religious heritage. Marriage and family responsibilities are discarded as impediments to personal indulgence. The movies and magazines and television that shape our attitudes are filled with stories or images that portray the children of God as predatory beasts or, at best, as trivial creations pursuing little more than personal pleasure. And too many of us accept this as entertainment.
>
> The men and women who made epic sacrifices to combat evil regimes in the past were shaped by values that are disappearing from our public teaching. The good, the true, and the beautiful are

> being replaced by the no-good, the "whatever," and the valueless fodder of personal whim. Not surprisingly, many of our youth and adults are caught up in pornography, pagan piercing of body parts, self-serving pleasure pursuits, dishonest behavior, revealing attire, foul language, and degrading sexual indulgence.
>
> An increasing number of opinion leaders and followers deny the existence of the God of Abraham, Isaac, and Jacob and revere only the gods of secularism. Many in positions of power and influence deny the right and wrong defined by divine decree. Even among those who profess to believe in right and wrong, there are "them that call evil good, and good evil" (Isa. 5:20; 2 Ne. 15:20).[19]

Comparing Elder Oaks' remarks to those made by the prophets cited above leaves little doubt that the worldly conditions foretold so long ago are indeed coming to pass. And with such an egregious and deep-rooted forgetting of God and His ways apparent on every hand, it is little wonder that He will take extraordinary measures to turn His wayward children from the path of eternal destruction.

A Desolating Scourge

The Lord calls upon the nations of the earth through His authorized emissaries to repent of their wickedness and come unto Him. The directive to lift up a warning voice is repeated several times in modern scripture.

> Lift up your voice as with the sound of a trump, both long and loud, and cry repentance unto a crooked and perverse generation, preparing the way of the Lord for His second coming. (D&C 34:6)
>
> Lift up your voices and spare not. Call upon the

> nations to repent, both old and young, both bond and free, saying: Prepare yourselves for the great day of the Lord. (D&C 43:20)
>
> Lift a warning voice unto the inhabitants of the earth; and declare . . . that desolation shall come upon the wicked. (D&C 63:37)

Serious consequences are bound to follow those who harden their hearts against the testimony of the Lord's authorized servants. Rejection of the Lord's call to repent can bring about "a desolating scourge," which "shall go forth among the inhabitants of the earth, and shall continue to be poured out from time to time, if they repent not" (D&C 5:18–19). In the vocabulary of Joseph Smith's day, the word scourge meant "to punish with severity; to chastise; to afflict for sins or faults . . . with the purpose of correction."[20] In one modern revelation, the Savior pronounces a "wo," or calamity, upon the house, village, or city that rejects the testimony of His servants concerning Him. The prospects for those who rebuff the message are grim, because the Lord has "laid [His] hands upon the nations, to scourge them for their wickedness" in the past and is prepared to do so again when circumstances call for it (D&C 84:92–96). In language that is unmistakably connected with Isaiah 28:18–19, Jesus Christ notifies the present generation with these words: "Vengeance cometh speedily upon the ungodly as the whirlwind; and who shall escape it? The Lord's scourge shall pass over by night and by day, and the report thereof shall vex all people; yea, it shall not be stayed until the Lord come. For the indignation of the Lord is kindled against their abominations and all their wicked works" (D&C 97:22–24). And again He raises the warning voice in modern revelation by announcing, "Mine indignation is soon to be poured out without measure upon all nations; and this will I do when the cup of their iniquity is full" (D&C 101:11). Divine fury is something best to be avoided, yet some of God's children will feel the sting of His scourge because of their stiff-necked adherence to the ways of a rebellious world.

The scourge of the Lord can take on many forms. A few that are mentioned in canonized scripture include wars (see D&C 63:33),[21] earthquakes in divers places (see D&C 43:25; 45:33; 88:89),[22] thunder and fierce lightning (see D&C 43:21–22, 25; 87:6; 88:90), tempests (see D&C 43:25; 88:90), desolating sickness (see D&C 45:31),[23] plagues (see D&C 84:96–97; 87:6),[24] famines (see D&C 43:25; 87:6), pestilences of every kind (D&C 43:25), great hailstorms (see D&C 29:16; 43:25),[25] and "the waves of the sea heaving themselves beyond their bounds" (D&C 88:90). In connection with the sign of heaving waves, the Lord reveals, "There are many dangers upon the waters" because He has "decreed in [His] anger many destructions upon the waters," and "the destroyer" rides upon their face (D&C 61:4–5, 19). This is a curse brought about in the last days but foreseen in ancient times by John the Revelator (D&C 61:14; cf. Revelation 8:8–11; 16:3–7).[26] When the Lord brought order out of chaos during the Creation of the earth, He established boundaries for the water (see Gen. 1:2, 6–7; Prov. 8:27–29). When water exceeds its bounds, that action can be interpreted symbolically as a reversal of the order of creation. Indeed, water—says the Lord in the book of Isaiah—is to be one of the elements utilized in the destruction of Babylon (see Isa. 14:22–23). Babylon, of course, will direct opposite of God's intended order of creation. Thus the water going beyond its limitations could be interpreted as a sign that the Lord's creation has gone outside its established boundary.

After Orson Hyde was ordained a member of the Quorum of the Twelve Apostles, he wrote in a Church periodical that among the signs or judgments of God will be serious losses caused by "whirlwinds and tempests, and devouring fire. The seasons [will also] be more irregular and uncertain in causing the earth to yield her bounty, for the sustenance of her inhabitants," he said.[27] Joseph Smith reaffirms that devouring fire will be a sign of the last days. In 1839 he mentioned a vision he was granted by the Lord wherein he witnessed "fires burning" before the Ancient of Days came to hold the great council at Adam-ondi-Ahman.[28]

The Lord's scourge will be used against the unrepentant, and the accustomed order of their lives will be greatly disturbed. The Lord Himself declares, "All things shall be in commotion; and surely, men's hearts shall fail them; for fear shall come upon all people" (D&C 88:91). The Lord also exclaims, "[There will be] many desolations; yet men will harden their hearts against me" (D&C 45:33). This prophecy evokes images of Moses' day, when the signs of God were worked against Pharaoh, but the Egyptian leader hardened his heart regardless (see JST, Ex. 7:10–13). The hardening of latter-day hearts will surely bring the same kind of appalling results that befell the ruler of Egypt.

Modern-day leaders of the Church of Jesus Christ have addressed the topic of the last days and their attendant signs, confirming the words of earlier prophets. President George Q. Cannon, who served as a counselor in the First Presidency, reflected:

> We are living in the last days. There is every indication that the words of the Lord are being fulfilled concerning judgments and calamities, wars and destructions. These things must come, and they will not be poured out without cause. God never punishes a people without first sending some message of warning to them. He never did in ancient days. Even Nineveh, guilty as it was, had the prophet Jonah sent to it to warn the inhabitants of their wickedness and exhort them to turn to God, and through their humiliation and repentance, humbling themselves before Him, clothing themselves, and even their animals, with sackcloth, and by sitting in ashes, the Lord averted the

> destruction He had threatened, and they escaped for that time. He has sent His messengers now to the nations of the earth; they have been going about . . . proclaiming the near approach of the day of the Lord. That day is coming and the judgments will be poured out. But will they be poured out without cause? No, they will not. It is because men reject God; it is because they will not accept the salvation that He proffers to them; it is because they will harden their hearts and reject the testimonies they might receive—it is on this account that these calamities will come. Yet when they do come those who witness them will not perceive in them the hand of God.[29]

President Gordon B. Hinckley acknowledged that this world "is no stranger to calamities and catastrophes," and remarked that "those of us who read and believe the scriptures are aware of the warnings of prophets concerning catastrophes that have come to pass and are yet to come to pass." Still, he admonished, "if anyone has any doubt concerning the terrible things that can and will afflict mankind, let him read the 24th chapter of Matthew." He further noted, "How interesting are descriptions of the tsunami and the recent hurricanes in terms of the language of [D&C 88:90], which says, 'The voice of the waves of the sea heaving themselves beyond their bounds.'" Even though "what we have experienced in the past was all foretold," President Hinckley declared, "the end is not yet. Just as there have been calamities in the past, we expect more in the future."[30]

With the unpleasant prospect of so many divine judgments coming upon the earth, the question naturally arises about how to avoid being overcome by them. The scriptures provide the answer to this question—in regard to the Saints as a people and also the Saints as individuals. Jesus Christ has indicated that in the day that

His indignation is poured out without measure, His covenant people Israel will be saved (D&C 101:10–12). When the Prophet Joseph Smith dedicated the Kirtland Temple in Ohio on March 27, 1836, he mentioned the outward mechanism for the salvation of the Lord's covenant people. He petitioned the Lord to withhold His judgments of wrath from the cities of the earth until the Saints had had the opportunity to enter them, proclaim His word of repentance, and gather out the righteous to Zion and her stakes (D&C 109:38–46). Indeed, the Lord has appointed the stakes of Zion as among those "holy places" where the Saints are to gather in order to "prepare for the revelation which is to come, when the veil of the covering of [the Lord's] temple, in [His] tabernacle, which hideth the earth, shall be taken off, and all flesh shall see [Him] together" (D&C 101:20–23). In Doctrine and Covenants 124, the Lord clearly states that a "refuge" for "the safety of [His] people" in the "day of [His] visitation" will be found in Zion (v. 6–11). The city of New Jerusalem in the state of Missouri, in particular, has been named as a place where the Saints can go for security.

> And it shall be called the New Jerusalem, a land of peace, a city of refuge, a place of safety for the Saints of the Most High God;
>
> And the glory of the Lord shall be there, and the terror of the Lord also shall be there, insomuch that the wicked will not come unto it, and it shall be called Zion.
>
> And it shall come to pass among the wicked, that every man that will not take his sword against his neighbor must needs flee unto Zion for safety.
>
> And there shall be gathered unto it out of every nation under heaven; and it shall be the only people that shall not be at war one with another. (D&C 45:66–69)

On a more individual level, the Lord places a qualification on the protection afforded to individual Saints who dwell in Zion and her stakes. To Orson Pratt the Lord said, "If you are *faithful*, behold, I am with you until I come" (D&C 34:11; emphasis added). To Thomas B. Marsh the admonition was the same: "Be *faithful* until I come, for I come quickly" (D&C 112:34; emphasis added). To Ezra Thayre and Northrop Sweet the instruction was repeated: "Wherefore, be *faithful*, praying always, having your lamps trimmed and burning, and oil with you, that you may be ready at the coming of the Bridegroom. For behold, verily, verily, I say unto you, that I come quickly" (D&C 33:17–18; emphasis added).[31]

Even with this general assurance, there is the chance that some of the Lord's dedicated disciples will still suffer during the prophesied occurrences of the last days. In Doctrine and Covenants 63, the Lord promises: "I, the Lord, am with them," but He also notes that "the Saints . . . will hardly escape" the consequences of the wars that will take place (v. 34). In the vernacular of the nineteenth century, the word *hardly* could mean "with difficulty, with great labor"; or "scarcely, barely, almost not"; or "not quite or wholly."[32] In the dedicatory prayer of the Kirtland Temple, the Prophet of the final dispensation addresses the Almighty in this manner: "We know that thou hast spoken by the mouth of thy prophets terrible things concerning the wicked, in the last days—that thou wilt pour out thy judgments, without measure; Therefore, O Lord, deliver thy people from the calamity of the wicked" and "prepare the hearts of thy saints for all those judgments thou art about to send, in thy wrath, upon the inhabitants of the earth, because of their transgressions, that thy people may not faint [or weaken, lose courage] in the day of trouble" (D&C 109:38, 45–46). This prophetic petition teaches that membership in the Church does not automatically shield an individual from the effects of God's judgments—but protection may be requested from Him.

The Prophet Joseph Smith also taught that there is no guarantee that every Saint will escape the penalties that will be inflicted upon a grossly wicked world:

> It is a false idea that the Saints will escape all the judgments whilst the wicked suffer for all flesh is subject to suffer and "the righteous shall hardly escape" [paraphrase of D&C 63:34]. Still, many of the Saints will escape for "the just shall live by faith" [Hab. 2:4; Rom. 1:17; Gal. 3:11; Heb. 10:38]. Yet many of the righteous shall fall a prey to disease, to pestilence, etc. by reason of the weakness of the flesh and *yet be saved in the kingdom of God*. . . . [I]t is an unhallowed principle to say that such and such [persons] have transgressed because they have been preyed upon by disease or death for all flesh is subject to death.[33]

Elder James E. Talmage, in trying to help the Latter-day Saints understand this concept, pointed out that it is not possible for mortals to always have an accurate knowledge of why some individuals have their lives taken during the outpouring of heavenly judgments. He explained:

> It is beyond the wisdom of men to correctly deduce results by applying general laws or causes to individual cases; and whenever the judgments of the Lord are permitted to fall upon the earth and upon its inhabitants, there are many of the innocent who suffer with the guilty. Many go down who are not personally culpable and who are not directly responsible for that which has come.
>
> We know the Lord does permit these calamities to come upon those who, according to our means of

> judgment and powers of analysis, may not have deserved the fate, but death, remember, is not finality. It is that which follows death with which we should have concern. Many are allowed to die in tempest and earthquake, whose death is but a passage into the blessed realms because they are deserving of blessings; while unto others death does come as a judgment; and the Lord knows who falls because of their sins and who are permitted to fall because of their righteousness.[34]

Mortals may rest assured that no matter what scourges may overtake the earth, they are being sent by a perfectly just and loving God who has the ultimate good of all His children in mind. As Elder Talmage states, the wisdom of mortals with regard to these affairs is insufficient. Therefore, it is advisable to solicit an accurate understanding of the reason and purpose behind signs on the earth from Him who knows all things.

Signs in the Heavens

When the Almighty desires to attract the attention of the earth's population, He not only causes signs to occur where they live but also in the direction of where He resides. Signs in the heavens can be identified as anything that happens above the plane of human habitation. Their purpose, however, is the same as those discussed in previous portions of this chapter: they are designed to confirm the Lord's existence and to encourage mankind to turn their thoughts to Him and their actions to righteousness.

Sun, Moon, and Stars

The prophet Joel foretells that one of the "wonders in the heavens" that will be visible "before the great and terrible day of the Lord" will be the sun turning into darkness and the moon turning into blood (Joel 2:30–31). The angel Moroni told the Prophet Joseph Smith that this prophecy had not yet been fulfilled but soon would be.[35] John the Revelator learned that this phenomenon takes place after Jesus Christ opens the sixth seal of the book of human history. John saw the sun become black and the moon become as blood. He also witnessed the stars falling to the earth (see Rev. 6:12–13). It should be noted that the Apostle John saw that after the Redeemer opened the seventh seal, another sun, moon, and stars phenomenon took place. "There fell a great star from heaven," says the text, "and the third part of the sun was smitten, and the third part of the moon, and the third part of the stars; so as the third part of them was darkened, and the day shone not for a third part of it, and the night likewise" (Rev. 8:1, 10–12). This second darkening of the heavenly bodies may occur because a dust cloud will be thrown up into the air by the falling of the star or meteorite just mentioned.

In latter-day revelation, the Savior confirmed that the first set of astronomical signs mentioned above will take place. In Doctrine and Covenants 29, for instance, He declares that "before [the] great day [of the Lord] shall come the sun shall be darkened, and the moon shall be turned into blood, and the stars shall fall from heaven" (v. 14; cf. D&C 45:42). Additional clarification is found in Doctrine and Covenants 34, which reveals that "the stars shall refuse their shining, and some shall fall" (v. 9). Also, in Doctrine and Covenants 88, the Lord explains that "the sun shall hide his face, and shall refuse to give light," "the moon shall be bathed in blood," and "the stars shall become exceedingly angry" and cast themselves down (v. 87).

The key to understanding this event seems to be the book of Joel. A careful study of chapters 2 and 3 (see Appendix 3 in this book) indicates that the context is the battle of Armageddon, which is described as "a day . . . of thick darkness" (Joel 2:2). A profitable comparison can be made between the material in the prophet Joel's writings and that which is found in the Book of Mormon in 3 Nephi. In connection with the first coming of Christ, these scriptural writings report, there was "thick darkness"; "there was not any light seen, . . . *neither the sun, nor the moon, nor the stars,* for so great were the mists of darkness which were upon the face of the land" (3 Ne. 8:19–23; emphasis added). In Joel's prophecy, the darkness could be interpreted as a result either of war or of divine action. In 3 Nephi, the darkness comes about because of divinely decreed natural disasters. In Ezekiel 32:1–9, a similar event is tied directly to a divine curse of the wicked, with the Lord prophesying the destruction of the leader of the Egyptians: "I will cover the heaven, and make the stars thereof dark; I will cover the sun with a cloud, and the moon shall not give her light. All the bright lights of heaven will I make dark over thee, and set darkness upon thy land, saith the Lord God."

Just as the chaotic force of water—mentioned above—hearkens back to the time of the Creation of the earth, so too can the darkness be understood in a similar way. When God brought order out of chaos in the first days of the Creation, He caused light to shine amid the darkness (see Gen. 1:2–3). Now, during the last days, He will reverse this action by bringing darkness upon the world. Overall, this seems to be another indication that God considers the gross wickedness present upon His earth to be contrary to His purpose in the Creation.

Absence of the Rainbow

After the destruction of the wicked by flood in the days of Noah, the Lord informed the ark-building patriarch and his sons about a covenant that He had established with the prophet Enoch. The Lord had promised Enoch that the earth would never again be destroyed by flood, and He now established that covenant with Noah (in behalf of "every living creature of all flesh"). The "token of the covenant" was designated as the rainbow in the cloud—a visual phenomenon produced through the mixture of water and light.The bow was also to serve as a reminder that when men keep all of God's commandments, He will send the city of Enoch or "Zion" back down to the earth. The "general assembly and Church of the Firstborn" will thus come down out of heaven and its inhabitants will have place on the earth "until the end" (JST, Gen. 9:15–25).

The rainbow is to play another significant role in the drama of the last days. This token of the world's preservation from destruction, said the Prophet Joseph Smith, will disappear prior to the time the earth is cleansed again. Through the power of revelation, the Prophet was taught the following truth, which he later recalled:

> I have asked of the Lord concerning His coming and while asking the Lord gave me a sign and said, "In the days of Noah I set a bow in the heavens as a sign and token that in any year that the bow should be seen the Lord would not come, but there should be seed time [and] harvest during that year. But whenever you see the bow withdraw, it shall be a token that there shall be famine, pestilence and great distress among the nations."[36]

The Prophet describes the absent rainbow as a portend of "desolation [and] calamity . . . [a period] without seed time and harvest."[37] It seems apparent that the sign of the absent rainbow is directly associated with the cycle of rain. What could interrupt this natural occurrence? There is a possibility that the cessation of rain will be connected with the two witnesses of the Lord who will prophesy in the city of Jerusalem for three and a half years, during the battle of Armageddon. Revelation 11:6 explicitly states that these two prophets "have power to shut heaven, that it rain not in the days of their prophecy." Famine and pestilence would surely follow after a lengthy season of drought.

The Sign of the Son of Man

Joseph Smith placed the appearance of the sign of the Son of Man after the sign of the absent rainbow in the chronology of the signs of the times.[38] He also placed this Messianic sign after the sun had been darkened and the moon bathed in blood.[39] Likewise, the Joseph Smith Translation of Matthew 24 states that "the sign of the Son of Man" will be seen in heaven after the days of tribulation and after "the powers of heaven" (or the stars) are "shaken" or fall from the sky (v. 37; cf. Rev. 6:13; D&C 88:87).

Just as a bright heavenly object announced the arrival of the Lord upon the earth during the meridian of time (see Matt. 2:1–2, 9–10), so too will His Second Coming be heralded. This "great sign" will be seen by "all people," and it will appear immediately after angels fly through the midst of heaven and announce the approach of the Bridegroom (see D&C 88:92–93). One of Joseph Smith's close associates, Wandle Mace, claimed that the Prophet said that this sign would be the return of the city of Enoch (cf. Moses 7:62–63).[40]

Joseph Smith provides valuable commentary on this subject, explaining that when this sign is seen by the world's population, they will speculate that "it is a planet, a comet, etc."[41] He also said that while the wicked will not understand its true significance—attributing it to a natural cause—the righteous will know what it means. And the coming of the Son of Man will be like the dawning of the morning sun that moves along gradually from the east until it reaches unto the west. In a manner similar to the sun, this sign will be small at first but will gradually increase until it is "all in a blaze" and every eye sees it.[42] Elder Orson Pratt was in agreement, teaching that "it is to be like our sun seen over one entire side of the globe, and then passing immediately round to the other, or else it will encircle the whole earth at the same time."[43] In either case, every eye will eventually behold this grand indication that something extraordinary is about to take place.

Additional Signs

Although the previously described signs are indeed miraculous, the Doctrine and Covenants asserts that there will be "greater signs in heaven above" than that of the stars falling, the sun being darkened, and the moon appearing as blood (D&C 29:14). President Wilford Woodruff, who was shown many of these additional signs by an angel of God, relates what one of them will be. As a missionary he had the following experience.

> I knelt down and prayed. I arose from my knees and sat down. The room was filled with light. A messenger came to me. We had a long conversation. He laid before me as if in a panorama, the signs of the last days, and told me what was coming to pass. I saw the sun turned to darkness, the moon to blood, [and] the stars fall from heaven. I saw the resurrection day. I saw armies of men in the first resurrection, clothed with the robes of the Holy Priesthood. I saw the second resurrection. I saw a great many signs that were presented before me [cf. Hel. 14:6], by this personage; and among the rest, there were seven lions, as of burning brass, set in the heavens. [The angel said], "That is one of the signs that will appear in the heavens before the coming of the Son of Man. It is a sign of the various dispensations."[44]

In another recital of this vision, President Woodruff again notes that these objects were "seven lions like burning brass placed in the heavens." He reports, "I asked the messenger what they were for. He said they were representative of the different dispensations of the gospel of Christ to men, and they would all be seen in the heavens among the signs that would be shown."[45]

During the early nineteenth century, Parley P. Pratt observed an unusual aerial sign that holds great significance to endowed Latter-day Saints. This future Apostle describes what he witnessed in his autobiographical writings:

> I had been on a visit to a singular people called Shakers, at New Lebanon, about seven miles from my aunt Van Cott's, and was returning that distance, on foot, on a beautiful evening of September [1830]. The sky was without a cloud; the stars shone out beautifully, and all nature seemed reposing in quiet, as I pursued my solitary way, wrapped in deep meditations on the predictions of the holy prophets; the signs of the times; the approaching advent of the Messiah to reign on the earth, and the important revelations of the Book of Mormon; my heart filled with gratitude to God that He had opened the eyes of my understanding to receive the truth, and with sorrow for the blindness of those who lightly rejected the same, when my attention was aroused by a sudden appearance of a brilliant light which shone around me, above the brightness of the sun. I cast my eyes upward to inquire from whence the light came, when I perceived a long chain of light extended in the heavens, very bright, and of a deep fiery red. It at first stood stationary in a horizontal position; at length bending in the center, the two ends approached each other with a rapid movement, so as to form an exact square. In this position it again remained stationary for some time, perhaps a minute, and then again the ends approached each other with the same rapidity, and again ceased to move, remaining stationary, for perhaps a minute,

> in the form of a compass; it then commenced a third movement in the same manner, and closed like the closing of a compass, the whole forming a straight line like a chain doubled. It again remained stationary for a minute, and then faded away.
>
> I fell upon my knees in the street, and thanked the Lord for so marvelous a sign of the coming of the Son of Man.
>
> Some persons may smile at this, and say that all these exact movements were by chance; but, for my part, I could as soon believe that the letters of the alphabet would be formed by chance, and be placed so as to spell my name, as to believe that these signs (known only to the wise) could be formed and shown forth by chance.[46]

On a most significant night, a final sign was seen in the heavens by Heber C. Kimball and other individuals. They witnessed this sign at the very time that the angel Moroni turned over the plates of the Book of Mormon to the Prophet Joseph Smith—September 22, 1827. Brother Kimball tells the story.

> I had retired to bed, when John P. Greene, who was living within a hundred steps of my house, came and [woke] me up, calling upon me to come out and behold the scenery in the heavens. I woke up and called my wife and Sister Fanny Young (sister to Brigham Young), who was living with us, and we went out-of-doors.
>
> It was one of the most beautiful starlight nights, so clear that we could see to pick up a pin. We looked to the eastern horizon, and beheld a white smoke arise toward the heavens; as it ascended it formed itself into a belt, and made a noise like the sound of a mighty

wind, and continued southwest, forming a regular bow dipping in the western horizon. After the bow had formed, it began to widen out and grow clear and transparent, of a bluish cast; it grew wide enough to contain twelve men abreast.

In this bow an army moved, commencing from the east and marching to the west; they continued marching until they reached the western horizon. They moved in platoons, and walked so close that the rear ranks trod in the steps of their file leaders, until the whole bow was literally crowded with soldiers. We could distinctly see the muskets, bayonets and knapsacks of the men, who wore caps and feathers like those used by the American soldiers in the last war with Britain; and also saw their officers with their swords and equipage, and the clashing and jingling of their implements of war [was heard], and [we] could discover the forms and features of the men. The most profound order existed throughout the entire army; when the foremost man stepped, every man stepped at the same time; I could hear the steps. When the front rank reached the western horizon a battle ensued, as we could distinctly hear the report of arms and the rush.

No man could judge of my feelings when I beheld that army of men, as plainly as ever I saw armies of men in the flesh; it seemed as though every hair of my head was alive. This scenery we gazed upon for hours, until it began to disappear.

After I became acquainted with Mormonism, I learned that this took place the same evening that Joseph Smith received the records of the Book of Mormon from the angel Moroni, who had held those records in his possession.

> John Young, Sen[ior], and John P. Greene's wife, Rhoda, were also witnesses.
>
> My wife, being frightened at what she saw, said, "Father Young, what does all this mean?"
>
> "Why, it's one of the signs of the coming of the Son of Man," he replied, in a lively, pleased manner.
>
> The next night similar scenery was beheld in the west by the neighbors, representing armies of men who were engaged in battle.[47]

Whether shown forth in the heavens above or on the earth beneath, the signs of the times are designed to reaffirm that these are the last days of decision and that future circumstances—even eternal destinies—will depend upon whether one chooses to stand with the righteous or fall with the wicked. "He that feareth me shall be looking forth for the great day of the Lord to come," said the Savior, "even for the signs of the coming of the Son of Man" (D&C 45:39).

Notes to Chapter 1

1. John R. Kohlenberger III and James A. Swanson, *The Strongest Strong's Exhaustive Concordance of the Bible* (Grand Rapids, MI: Zondervan, 2001), 1357, Hebrew-Aramaic Dictionary, word #226; hereafter cited as *SSECB.*

2. Ibid., 1411, Hebrew-Aramaic Dictionary, word #4159.

3. Ibid., 1449, Hebrew-Aramaic Dictionary, word #6963.

4. Joseph F. Smith, *Gospel Doctrine* (Salt Lake City: Deseret Book, 1986), 55.

5. Bruce R. McConkie, *A New Witness for the Articles of Faith* (Salt Lake City: Deseret Book, 1985), 623; hereafter cited as *NWAF.*

6. CR, Apr. 1951, 41.

7. *NWAF,* 630.

8. James E. Talmage, *A Study of the Articles of Faith* (Salt Lake City: The Church of Jesus Christ of Latter-day Saints, 1950), 17; hereafter cited as *SAF.*

9. *JD,* 12:354; ibid., 22:93; Eliza R. Snow, *Biography and Family Record of Lorenzo Snow* (Salt Lake City: Deseret News Press, 1884), 137.

10. *Messenger and Advocate,* vol. 2, no. 13, Oct. 1835, 199; emphasis added; hereafter cited as *MA.*

11. *T&S,* vol. 3, no. 12, 15 Apr. 1842, 753.

12. *MA,* vol. 1, no. 7, Apr. 1835, 111–12.

13. *HC* 1:357–62.

14. Andrew F. Ehat and Lyndon W. Cook, ed., *The Words of Joseph Smith: The Contemporary Accounts of the Nauvoo Discourses of the Prophet Joseph* (Provo, UT: BYU Religious Studies Center, 1980), 417; hereafter cited as *WJS.*

15. Ibid., 180. Apostle Orson Hyde dedicated and consecrated the city of Jerusalem on October 24, 1841, for the rebuilding of the temple there (see *T&S,* vol. 3, no. 11, 1 Apr. 1842, 740–41). On April 6, 1845, the Quorum of the Twelve Apostles issued a proclamation to the rulers of the earth wherein they made it

known that the Jews among all nations were commanded, in the name of the Messiah, to prepare to return to Jerusalem and rebuild the temple there. They made it clear in this document that they held "the keys of the priesthood and kingdom which [was] soon to be restored unto them" and that the Jews needed to "prepare to obey the ordinances of God"—meaning "the endowment and ordinances pertaining to the priesthood," which the Twelve Apostles alone had authority to administer and which were designed to prepare recipients "for the coming of the Lord" (James R. Clark, comp., *Messages of the First Presidency of The Church of Jesus Christ of Latter-day Saints* [Salt Lake City: Bookcraft, 1965–1975], 1:254–55; hereafter cited as *MFP*).

16. *NWAF*, 586–87. Elder McConkie has asserted elsewhere: "Judah will gather to old Jerusalem in due course; of this, there is no doubt. But this gathering will consist of accepting Christ, joining the Church, and receiving anew the Abrahamic covenant as it is administered in holy places. The present assembling of people of Jewish ancestry into the Palestinian nation of Israel is not the scriptural gathering of Israel or of Judah. It may be prelude thereto, and some of the people so assembled may in due course be gathered into the true Church and kingdom of God on earth, and they may then assist in building the temple that is destined to grace Jerusalem's soil. But a political gathering is not a spiritual gathering, and the Lord's kingdom is not of this world" (ibid., 519–20).

17. Neal A. Maxwell, *Look Back at Sodom* (Salt Lake City: Deseret Book, 1975), 13.

18. *MFP,* 2:64.

19. *Ensign,* May 2004, 9–10.

20. Noah Webster, *An American Dictionary of the English Language* (New York: S. Converse, 1828), s.v. "scourge," definition 2; hereafter cited as *ADEL.*

21. In Doctrine and Covenants 63:33–34, the Lord states: "I have sworn in my wrath, and decreed wars upon the face of the

earth, and the wicked shall slay the wicked, and fear shall come upon every man; And the Saints also shall hardly [i.e., with difficulty, barely, not wholly] escape." The Lord has also prophesied that "the time will come that war will be poured out upon all nations. . . . Thus, with the sword and by bloodshed the inhabitants of the earth shall mourn . . . [and] the inhabitants of the earth [will] be made to feel the wrath, and indignation, and chastening hand of an Almighty God, until the consumption decreed hath made a full end of all nations" (D&C 87:2, 6). In commenting upon the material found in Matthew 24, the Lord explains that "in that day [when the times of the Gentiles is fulfilled and a remnant of scattered Israel is gathered] shall be heard of *wars and rumors of wars*" (D&C 45:24–26; emphasis added). The prophet Nephi provides keys to interpret this prophecy and thus understand the nature of these wars. Nephi was shown a vision wherein he saw that when the wrath of God was poured out upon the great and abominable church or mother of harlots, then "there began to be *wars and rumors of wars* among all the nations which belonged to the mother of abominations" (1 Ne. 14:15–16; emphasis added). The nations that will be involved in this warfare are identified by Nephi as being "every nation which shall war against . . . [the] house of Israel." These nations, which belong to "that great and abominable church, which is the whore of all the earth . . . shall war among themselves, and the sword of their own hands shall fall upon their own heads"; they "shall be turned one against another." Ultimately, "all that fight against Zion shall be destroyed, and that great whore, who hath perverted the right ways of the Lord, yea, that great and abominable church, shall tumble to the dust and great shall be the fall of it" (1 Ne. 22:13–14).

22. When D&C 45:48, 49:23, and 88:87 are considered together, it appears that an earthquake occasioned by the Lord's descent on the Mount of Olives will be what causes the earth to "reel to and fro" like a drunken man (cf. Isa. 24:20).

23. Early members of the LDS Church viewed sicknesses such as influenza and cholera as "signs of the times" (*HC* 1:347–48).

24. The First Presidency of the Church in 1851, consisting of Brigham Young, Heber C. Kimball, and Willard Richards, issued an epistle predicting that "the overflowing scourges of God's wrath shall destroy the nations, and depopulate the earth on account of the multiplied infidelity and abominations of the inhabitants thereof. . . . The increasing plagues and sickness in new and diversified forms, baffling the skill of the ablest physicians, and causing the wisdom of their wisest to perish . . . all these signs, and . . . many more like things [are the fulfillment of prophecies which] should come to pass in this generation, as signs of the second coming of the Son of Man" (*MFP*, 2:63–64).

25. The reference in D&C 29:16 is to a single "great hailstorm sent forth to destroy the crops of the earth." The shortage of food that will result from this catastrophe gives Latter-day Saints ample reason to seriously consider Church leaders' counsel to store a reserve of edible provisions. President Gordon B. Hinckley has advised the Saints to set aside some food in case of emergency, but he has also cautioned "not [to] panic or go to extremes" in this matter (Gordon B. Hinckley, *Discourses of Gordon B. Hinckley, Volume 2: 2000–2004* [Salt Lake City: Deseret Book, 2005], 109).

26. On August 9, 1831 (the day before Doctrine and Covenants 61 was received), William W. Phelps learned of the reality of the Lord's curse on the waters when he "in open vision by daylight, saw the destroyer in his most horrible power, ride upon the face of the waters; others heard the noise, but saw not the vision" (*HC* 1:203). The Lord notes that the "faithful" or "upright in heart" will be preserved upon the waters so that they will not perish (D&C 61:6, 16). There will be instances when certain individuals will be "given power to command the waters," supposedly for the sake of preserving life while traveling upon them (v. 27–28).

27. *MA,* vol. 2, no. 22, July 1836, 345. The First Presidency of the Church in 1851 included the "increase of . . . hurricanes [and] tornadoes" among the signs of the times (*MFP,* 2:63).

28. *WJS,* 11.

29. Brian H. Stuy, ed., *Collected Discourses* (Burbank, CA: B.H.S. Publishing, 1987), 1:299; hereafter cited as *CD.*

30. *Ensign,* Nov. 2005, 61–62. After providing a list of the signs of the times, Dallin H. Oaks notes, "These signs of the second coming are all around us and seem to be increasing in frequency and intensity. For example, the list of major earthquakes in *The World Almanac and Book of Facts, 2004* shows twice as many earthquakes in the decades of the 1980s and 1990s as in the two preceding decades (pp. 189–90). It also shows further sharp increases in the first several years of this century. The list of notable floods and tidal waves and the list of hurricanes, typhoons, and blizzards worldwide show similar increases in recent years (pp. 188–89). Increases by comparison with 50 years ago can be dismissed as changes in reporting criteria, but the accelerating pattern of natural disasters in the last few decades is ominous" (ibid., May 2004, 7–8).

31. Wilford Woodruff taught the same basic principle when he said that those people who have "a right to be shielded" against the great calamities and judgments of the last days are those who honor the priesthood and stand worthy of its blessings. Yet he acknowledged that "not even this people [i.e., the Latter-day Saints] will escape [the calamities and judgments] entirely" (*Young Woman's Journal,* vol. 5, no. 11, Aug. 1894, 512). President John Taylor expressed similar thoughts: "The judgments will begin at the house of God. We have to pass through some of these things, but it will only be a very little compared with the terrible destruction, the misery and suffering that will overtake the world who are doomed to suffer the wrath of God. It behooves us, as the Saints of God, to stand firm and faithful in the observance of His laws, that we may be worthy of His preserving care and blessing" (*JD,*

21:100). Likewise, Elder Bruce R. McConkie noted that "we do not say that all of the Saints will be spared and saved from the coming day of desolation. But we do say there is no promise of safety . . . except for those who love the Lord and who are seeking to do all that He commands. It may be, for instance, that nothing except the power of faith and the authority of the priesthood can save individuals and congregations" (CR, Apr. 1979, 132–33). The doctrine of deliverance from the calamities of the last days through calling upon the name of the Lord is clearly taught in Joel 2:31–32. The Savior Himself says in JST, Luke 21:36, "What I say unto one, I say unto all, Watch ye therefore, and pray always, and keep my commandments, that ye may be counted worthy to escape all these things which shall come to pass, and to stand before the Son of Man when He shall come clothed in the glory of His Father."

32. Webster, *ADEL,* s.v., "hardly," definitions 1–3.

33. *WJS,* 15; emphasis added.

34. CR, October 1923, 51–52.

35. See *T&S,* vol. 3, no. 12, 15 April 1842, 753.

36. *WJS,* 332. Included among the great distress to be found among the nations, according to Joseph Smith, will be "wars" (ibid., 335). The Prophet was very specific in stating that the sign of the missing rainbow does not apply to anything except that which is seen "stretching across the heavens" (ibid., 334) or "in the cloud" (ibid., 335).

37. Ibid., 336.

38. See ibid., 335.

39. See *HC* 5:291.

40. Wandle Mace statement located in the "Joseph Smith Papers" collection, LDS Church Archives, Salt Lake City, Utah.

41. *WJS,* 180.

42. Ibid., 181.

43. *JD,* 8:50.

44. *CD,* 1:217.

45. Ibid., 5:236.

46. Parley P. Pratt, *Autobiography of Parley P. Pratt,* rev. ed. (Salt Lake City: Deseret Book, 2000), 42.

47. Orson F. Whitney, *Life of Heber C. Kimball* (Salt Lake City: Bookcraft, 1967), 15–17.

CHAPTER 2
THE SECOND COMING

According to LDS scriptural texts, the Lord Jesus Christ, before He appears to the entire world in power and great glory, will make several preliminary appearances on the earth. This chapter discusses the appearances that will occur at Adam-ondi-Ahman, at the temple of the American Zion in New Jerusalem, and to a group of Israelites on the Mount of Olives. Additionally, the doctrinal concepts associated with the coming of the Lord to the entire world will be presented.

Adam-ondi-Ahman

The Savior, through latter-day revelation, has explained that an Old Testament prophecy by Daniel concerning the Ancient of Days (or Adam) coming to visit his people (see Dan. 7:9–14) will be fulfilled at a place called Adam-ondi-Ahman, which is located in the state of Missouri (see D&C 116:1). This event will follow the same overall pattern of a council that was held three years before Adam died, which is described in Doctrine and Covenants 107: "Three years previous to the death of Adam, he called Seth, Enos, Cainan, Mahalaleel, Jared, Enoch, and Methuselah, who were all high priests, with the residue of his posterity who were righteous, into the valley of Adam-ondi-Ahman, and there bestowed upon them his last blessing. And the Lord appeared unto them" (v. 53–54).

According to the Prophet Joseph Smith, the appearance of the Lord at Adam-ondi-Ahman in the last days will occur sometime prior to the coming of the Son of Man to the entire world. This event is, in fact, designed as a preparation for that worldwide visitation.[1] Other statements by Joseph Smith help clarify the issue of chronology. On one occasion the Prophet spoke of "war, and fires burning, [and] earthquake, one pestilence after another, etc. until the Ancient of Days come[s] then judgment will be given to the Saints."[2] Thus, the coming of Adam occurs after a period of great tribulation. The reference to war is explained somewhat by the Prophet's reference at another time to the book of Daniel. The Prophet declared: "The horn [which was the symbol of a king] made war with the Saints, and overcame them etc., until the Ancient of Days came. Judgment was [then] given to the Saints of the Most High, from the Ancient of Days—[in other words,] the time came that the Saints possessed the kingdom."[3] The council, then, takes place at the end of a period of persecution against the Saints. The appearance of the Lord can be placed in its proper chronological sequence by consulting the prophecy of Daniel, which specifies that the Ancient of Days and the Son of Man will meet after "thrones [are] cast down" (Dan. 7:9). Elder Orson Pratt refers to this era when he says that "this prophecy relates to a period of time in the history of our race, when thrones are to be cast down, when kingdoms and the various governments which exist upon the face of the earth are to be overthrown."[4]

The dissolving of earthly kingdoms is the central reason for the meeting of the council at Adam-ondi-Ahman. "Until this grand council is held," explained Joseph Fielding Smith, "Satan shall hold rule in the nations of the earth; but at that time thrones are to be cast down and man's rule shall come to an end—for it is decreed that the Lord shall make an end of all nations (see D&C 87:6)."[5] It is during this council—held at a place where the Lord once acknowledged the royal status of Adam (see D&C 107:53–54) that "our Savior shall be crowned King of kings and take His place as the rightful ruler of the earth."[6] This acknowledgment of the Lord's right to reign will occur through the reporting of key-holder stewardships back to the Messiah. Joseph Smith teaches this concept:

> The priesthood was first given to Adam: he obtained the first Presidency and held the keys of it from generation to generation. . . . He had dominion given him over every living creature. He is Michael, the archangel. . . . Noah, who is Gabriel, . . . stands next in authority to Adam in the priesthood. . . . To him was given the dominion. These men held keys. . . . The keys have to be brought from heaven whenever the gospel is sent [or restored]. When they are revealed from heaven it is by Adam's authority.
>
> Daniel [in chapter] seven [of his book] speaks of the Ancient of Days—he means the oldest man, our Father Adam [or] Michael; he will call his children together and hold a council with them to prepare them for the coming of the Son of Man. He (Adam) is the father of the human family and presides over the spirits of all men, and all that have had the keys must stand before him in this great council. . . . The Son of Man [then] stands before [Adam] and there is given [to the Son] glory and dominion. Adam delivers up his stewardship to Christ, that which was delivered to him as holding the keys of the universe, but retains his standing as head of the human family. . . .
>
> Those men to whom these keys have been given will have to be there [at Adam-ondi-Ahman when the Ancient of Days comes].[7]

Elder John Taylor, who spoke personally with the Prophet concerning these matters, describes those persons who are to assemble as Adam's "children of the priesthood."[8] Elder Taylor further relates that as a result of their conversations he knew that President Smith was speaking of "the various dispensations and of those holding the keys thereof, and [Joseph] said there would then be a general giving up or accounting for." In other words, the Prophet Joseph stated that the key-holders would "deliver up or give an account of their administrations, in their several dispensations, but that they would all retain their several positions and Priesthood" after the meeting had taken place.[9]

Who else will attend this great council meeting? Elder Orson Pratt believes that the "ten thousand times ten thousand" (or 100 million) people who Daniel said would stand before the Ancient of Days at this meeting will be those who are "immortal beings"[10] or, put another way, a "vast multitude from the heavens."[11] Nevertheless, "when this gathering is held, the world will not know of it; the members of the Church at large will not know of it," said Joseph Fielding Smith. Only those "who officially shall be called . . . into this council [will be aware of its occurrence] for it shall precede the coming of Jesus Christ as a thief in the night, unbeknown to all the world."[12]

There are three other major appearances by the Lord that are associated with the Second Coming. When Ezra Taft Benson held the position of President of the Quorum of the Twelve Apostles, he established the following chronology:

> [Christ's] first appearance will be to the righteous Saints who have gathered to the New Jerusalem. In this place of refuge they will be safe from the wrath of the Lord, which will be poured out without measure on all nations. . . .
>
> The second appearance of the Lord will be to the Jews. To these beleaguered sons of Judah,

> surrounded by hostile Gentile armies, who again threaten to overrun Jerusalem, the Savior—their Messiah—will appear and set His feet on the Mount of Olives, "and it shall cleave in twain, and the earth shall tremble, and reel to and fro, and the heavens also shall shake" (D&C 45:48). The Lord Himself will then rout the Gentile armies, decimating their forces (see Ezek. 38, 39). . . .
>
> The third appearance of Christ will be to the rest of the world.[13]

Because the three appearances mentioned by President Benson have such a central role in the prophecies of the last days, they will receive individual treatment in the remainder of this chapter, with particular emphasis on the final one in the sequence.

New Jerusalem

In the due time of the Lord, the city of Zion will be built up in Jackson County, Missouri, and a magnificent temple constructed within its boundaries (see D&C 57:1–5; 84:4; 136:18). The Prophet Joseph Smith explains that this will occur sometime before the Second Coming: "Zion and Jerusalem must both be built up before the coming of Christ . . . and when these cities are built then shall the coming of the Son of Man be."[14]

In 1845, the Quorum of the Twelve Apostles—in an official proclamation—affirmed that the future city of Zion will be a temple city and also a "seat of government," because the Lord's "throne" will be found there. "It will be to the western hemisphere what Jerusalem will be to the eastern," they said.[15]

The city of Zion in the state of Missouri is referred to as both "New Jerusalem" and "Mount Zion" in modern-day revelation. The Savior revealed, in regard to the New Jerusalem temple, that a "cloud" or "the glory of the Lord" will rest upon it and also fill it (D&C 84:2–5). In speaking specifically of this temple in "the land of Zion," the Savior stated that as long as this temple remains undefiled, not only will His "glory . . . rest upon it" but His "presence shall be there, for [He] will come into it, and all the pure in heart that shall come into it shall see God" (D&C 97:10, 15–17). In Doctrine and Covenants 42, the Savior confirms that He will come to His temple, which is located in "New Jerusalem" (see v. 35–36).

These scriptures, however, do not speak of a formal appearance to a large group of assembled Saints—as when the Nephites saw the Lord as they stood outside the temple in the land of Bountiful (see 3 Ne. 11:1–11). Doctrine and Covenants 97 suggests, rather, a number of appearances to worthy persons who *enter* the New Jerusalem temple. A statement made by Elder Orson Pratt also seems to limit this type of event to either personal appearances or small group appearances. In alluding to this section of the Doctrine and Covenants, Elder Pratt says that

> All of them who are pure in heart will behold the face of the Lord and that too before He comes in His glory in the clouds of heaven, for He will suddenly come to His temple, and He will purify the sons of Moses and of Aaron [i.e, priesthood holders—see D&C 84:31–32], until they shall be prepared to offer in that temple an offering that shall be acceptable in the sight of the Lord. In doing this, He will purify not only the minds of the priesthood in that temple, but He will purify their bodies until they shall be quickened, renewed and strengthened, and they will be partially changed, not to immortality, but changed in part that they can be filled with the power of God, and they can stand in the presence of Jesus, and behold His face in the midst of that temple.[16]

Elder Pratt noted on another occasion that the Lord Jesus Christ will visit the New Jerusalem temple "occasionally" in order to reign upon His throne as King of Kings and Lord of Lords—just as He will from His throne at Old Jerusalem.[17] Therefore, it seems that the Lord will show Himself on many occasions to Saints in the New Jerusalem temple. This view coincides with the words of Charles W. Penrose, who said that Jesus Christ "will come to the temple prepared for Him, and His faithful people will behold His face, hear His voice, and gaze upon His glory. From His own lips they will receive further instructions for the development and beautifying of Zion and for the extension and sure stability of His kingdom."[18]

One of the most intriguing subjects related to the latter-day coming of the Lord is the 144,000 individuals who will stand with Him on Mount Zion. In Doctrine and Covenants 133, the Messiah proclaims: "Prepare ye the way of the Lord, and make His paths straight, for the hour of His coming is nigh—When the Lamb shall stand upon Mount Zion, and with Him a hundred and forty-four thousand, having His Father's name written on their foreheads" (v. 17–18). This scriptural passage draws upon imagery found in the New Testament book of Revelation. After the sixth seal of the book held by Jesus Christ was opened in John's Apocalypse, the Apostle saw a representation of four angels standing at the four corners of the earth. A fifth angel, who possessed "the seal of the living God," appeared in the east and cried out to the other four, "Hurt not the earth, neither the sea, nor the trees, till we have sealed the servants of our God in their foreheads" (Rev. 7:1–3). John then heard a voice declare that 12,000 people had been sealed out of each of the twelve tribes of Israel—totaling 144,000 individuals (see v. 4–8). Later in this vision, John was shown a representation of the 144,000 sealed individuals standing with the "Lamb," or Jesus Christ, on Mount Zion. This group sang a "new song" before God's throne, a song which only this group was able to learn (see Rev. 14:1–3).

The identity of the 144,000 can be better understood by examining the scriptural texts that describe their characteristics, and also by turning to commentary by latter-day Apostles and prophets. The book of Revelation indicates that the 144,000 "follow the Lamb" (Rev. 14:4); are "the servants . . . of God" (Rev. 7:3); are an elect group, the only people that can obtain a certain type of knowledge (see Rev. 14:2–3); and are "redeemed from the earth" (Rev. 14:3) or "redeemed from among men" (Rev. 14:4), suggesting that they have been cleansed by the Atonement. In addition, it is said that they have no "guile" (Rev. 14:5), are "not defiled" morally (Rev. 14:4), and are "without fault before the throne of God"—meaning that they have been judged and found worthy (Rev. 14:5). These individuals are the "firstfruits unto God and the Lamb"—meaning that they qualify for a celestial resurrection (Rev. 14:4; cf. D&C 88:97–98). They are standing upon Mount Zion, which is the name of the mountain where the temple stood in ancient Israel (see Rev. 14:1). They have been sealed in their foreheads (see Rev. 7:3) and also have God the Father's name written in or on their foreheads (see Rev. 14:1; cf. D&C 133:18).

Joseph Smith offers further insight on the 144,000 through his public statements. In Doctrine and Covenants 77, for instance, he indicates that the 144,000 sealed individuals are "high priests" from all nations who have been "ordained unto the holy order of God." Their purpose is "to administer the everlasting gospel" and "to bring as many as will come to the church of the Firstborn" (D&C 77:11).

In referring specifically to the passages in the book of Revelation under discussion, the Prophet Joseph Smith revealed that "where it says, 'and they shall seal the servants of God in their foreheads,' etc. it means to seal the blessing on their heads meaning the everlasting covenant thereby making their calling and election sure."[19] More precisely, this refers to the "sealing of the servants of God on the top of their heads."[20] The Prophet also spoke of "the necessity of the temple that the servants of God may be sealed in their foreheads."[21]

On one occasion Joseph Smith spoke of the 144,000 as "saviors on Mount Zion."[22] Orson F. Whitney offers a valuable perspective on this title:

> There is but one Savior; there is only "one name given under heaven whereby men can be saved" [see Acts 4:12]; but there may be innumerable assistants, innumerable subordinates, saviors in a lesser sense and degree. John the Revelator saw no less than one hundred and forty-four thousand of such saviors, standing on the Mount Zion, with the Father's name written in their foreheads; and it was said of them, "These are they that follow the Lamb whithersoever He goeth" [Rev. 14:4].[23]

Joseph Smith explained that saviors on Mount Zion are those people who are able to "redeem" the dead (thus imitating the Savior Jesus Christ) by "receiving all the [temple] ordinances" by proxy that are necessary so that those beyond the veil can "come forth in the first resurrection and be exalted to thrones of glory."[24] The theme of exaltation is also mentioned in Revelation 14:1. This scripture reports that the 144,000 have the name of God the Father written in their foreheads. Modern Apostles such as John Taylor,[25] Orson Pratt,[26] and Bruce R. McConkie[27] are united in the view that the Father's name in these individuals' foreheads signifies that they qualify for godhood. The fact that the 144,000 are tasked with bringing others into the Church of the Firstborn (see D&C 77:11) is significant because the Church of the Firstborn is the heavenly church of those who qualify for exaltation.[28]

As for the number 144,000 itself, one respected LDS scholar points out that "the number need not be taken literally." He admonishes us to "note that [Joseph Smith's commentary in D&C 77:11] does not specify a number. Instead it notes that the group is composed of high priests who have a special calling 'to administer the everlasting gospel' and 'to bring as many as will come to the church of the Firstborn.'" The symbolic meaning of the number, says this commentator, "supports this association. Twelve represents the priesthood. Biblical people squared a number to amplify its symbolic meaning. Thus, 144 suggests a fullness of priesthood authority. But John is not satisfied with that. He gives the image a superlative quality by multiplying [by] 1,000, representing completeness. In this way he shows the strength and breadth of the priesthood in the latter days."[29] Indeed, the Prophet Joseph Smith refers to the period of the last days as "the dispensation of the fullness of the priesthood,"[30] and the Lord stated that "the fulness of the priesthood" will be available to the Saints inside the temple (D&C 124:28). On April 2, 1843, the Prophet directly identified the 144,000 as temple priests.[31] On another occasion he said that the 144,000 on Mount Zion are part of "a kingdom of priests and kings."[32] And on February 4, 1844, he indicated that "the selection of persons to form that number ha[s] already commenced" in the dispensation of the fulness of times.[33]

Old Jerusalem

In Doctrine and Covenants 45, the Lord declares that Zechariah 13 and 14 include prophecies connected with His coming to the Jews during the battle of Armageddon. Doctrine and Covenants 45 and Revelation 16 also help define which prophecies regarding the last days will be fulfilled during this timeframe.

The battle of Armageddon, as described in the book of Revelation, will be incited by three evil spirits who will work some unspecified miracles among the leaders of the earth to convince them to fight against Israel (see Rev. 16:13–14, 16). In referring to John's meridian revelation, Elder Melvin J. Ballard of the Quorum of the Twelve Apostles teaches: "John saw a day when the righteous forces, both living and dead, shall be arrayed in a deadly conflict, at a place which he called Armageddon, against the forces of evil, both living and dead, to settle the question of supremacy in the earth. The forces of evil are at work preparing for that conflict. The evil one has his recruiting stations open everywhere, enlisting souls in the vain hope that he may yet gain the victory and obtain permanent right of rulership in the earth."[34] Zechariah 14 tells of this event—a time when the city of Jerusalem will be engaged in a battle against "all nations" that have been gathered against it. When half of the city has been taken captive, the Lord will descend along with "all the Saints" upon the Mount of Olives, which will be divided on an east-west axis, with one-half moving to the north and the other toward the south (v. 4–5). In Doctrine and Covenants 45:48, the Lord adds that an enormous earthquake will accompany this occurrence, an earthquake so powerful that it will seem like the heavens themselves shake. Indeed, Revelation 16:18 refers to this "great earthquake" and defines it as the worst that has occurred since mankind first inhabited the earth. In consequence of this quake, the cities of the nations will fall, islands will flee, mountains will disappear, and the city of Jerusalem will be divided into three parts (v. 19–20).

Furthermore, the Doctrine and Covenants foretells that after the earthquake, "the Lord shall utter His voice, and all the ends of the earth shall hear it; and the nations of the earth shall mourn, and they that have laughed shall see their folly. And calamity shall cover the mocker, and the scorner shall be consumed; and they that have watched for iniquity shall be hewn down and cast into the fire" (D&C 45:49–50). It appears from this passage that at this time the Lord will give a vocal command and cause the enemies of the Israelites to be destroyed. The prophet Zechariah relates the particulars of how the scorner will be consumed. "And this shall be the plague wherewith the Lord will smite all the people that have fought against Jerusalem; Their flesh shall consume away while they stand upon their feet, and their eyes shall consume away in their holes [i.e., sockets], and their tongue shall consume away in their mouth" (Zech. 14:12).

Apparently, yet another plague will decimate the enemies of the Lord's people at this time. John the Revelator describes this bitter trial: "And there fell upon men a great hail out of heaven, every stone about the weight of a talent: and men blasphemed God because of the plague of the hail; for the plague thereof was exceeding great" (Rev. 16:21).

Elder Parley P. Pratt provides a summary of some of the events connected with the battle of Armageddon:

> [T]he Jews gather home, and rebuild Jerusalem. The nations gather against them to battle. Their armies encompass the city, and have more or less power over it for three years and a half. A couple of . . . prophets, by their mighty miracles, keep them from utterly overcoming the Jews; until at length they are slain, and the city is left in a great measure to the mercy of their enemies for three days and a half. The two prophets rise from the dead and ascend up into heaven. The Messiah comes, convulses the earth, overthrows the army of the Gentiles, delivers the Jews, [and] cleanses Jerusalem.[35]

Joseph Smith teaches that the two prophets who will prophesy in Jerusalem and sacrifice their lives will be "*raised up to* the Jewish nation in the last days" (D&C 77:15; emphasis added), so the possibility exists that the prophets themselves will not be of Jewish ancestry. It is Elder LeGrand Richards' teaching that undoubtedly "these prophets will be called and ordained and sent by the First

Presidency of The Church of Jesus Christ of Latter-day Saints, for the Lord's house is a house of order, and true prophets are never self sent—they must be called and sent of God."[36] Likewise, Elder Bruce R. McConkie states that these two individuals "will be members of the Council of the Twelve or of the First Presidency of the Church."[37]

The valley formed by the division of the Mount of Olives when the Redeemer arrives will serve as an escape route for the surviving Israelites, and they will flee into it (see Zech. 14:5). The Lord, in Doctrine and Covenants 45, foretells what will happen next, an episode that will be one of the most profound moments in all of human history:

> And then shall the Jews look upon me and say: "What are these wounds in thine hands and in thy feet?"
>
> Then shall they know that I am the Lord; for I will say unto them: "These wounds are the wounds with which I was wounded in the house of my friends. I am He who was lifted up. I am Jesus that was crucified. I am the Son of God."
>
> And then shall they weep because of their iniquities; then shall they lament because they persecuted their king. (v. 51–53; cf. Zech. 13:6)

As mentioned previously, the Lord will not be alone when He descends upon the Mount of Olives to rescue the Jews in their time of great peril. When Jesus Christ ascended from that very same location after His first advent, two angels appeared there to testify that He would come again in like manner someday (see Acts 1:9–12). The presence of the Messiah and "all the Saints" on the Mount of Olives in the last days helps to explain an enigmatic statement made in Zechariah's writings. He mentions that "in that day [when the Lord comes with the Saints] . . . at evening time it shall be light" (Zech. 14:6–7). The Book of Mormon tells us that when the Savior came to the earth the first time, a night without darkness served as a sign of His coming (Hel. 14:1–4; 3 Ne. 1:14–15, 19). In the case of the Lord appearing on the Mount of Olives, the light that illuminates the darkness may be supplied by the Savior Himself and the innumerable celestial beings who accompany Him, the brightness radiating directly from their glorified bodies (cf. Rev. 21:23; Acts 12:7).

In Power and Great Glory

Most Christians think of the Second Coming as the appearance of the Savior to the entire population of the earth, an event that "surely shall come" (D&C 39:21).

Modern revelation confirms that no mortal knows the exact time when the Second Coming will take place—"neither the day nor the hour" (D&C 133:11). Not even the angels in heaven are privy to this information; in fact, they will not be made aware of it until it actually happens (see D&C 49:7). At the beginning of the dispensation of the fulness of times, the Lord announced only that the Second Coming will take place "by and by" (D&C 63:34–35), or, as He states, it will occur "in [His] own due time" (D&C 43:29). Nevertheless, scriptural forewarnings assure that it is near (see D&C 35:15; 43:17), that it will take place at an hour that mankind thinks not (see D&C 51:20; 61:38; JST, Matt. 24:51), and it will come "speedily" or "quickly" (D&C 124:10; 33:18). But although it will overtake the world, in general, as a thief in the night (see 2 Pet. 3:10), the Lord's latter-day disciples are admonished to become "children of light" so that this day will not overtake them as a thief (D&C 106:4–5; cf. 1 Thes. 5:4–5). Elder Orson Pratt, while acknowledging that the day and the hour of the Second Coming are a secret, believes that "there may be men that will know within a year—that will have revelation to say within one or two years when the Lord shall appear. I do not know that there is anything against this."[38] Indeed, the Prophet Joseph Smith himself allowed for the possibility of an advance notification of the Second Coming, citing Amos 3:7 for support of the idea. He also pointed to the sign of the Son of Man as a visible witness to the Saints that the Second Coming is very close at hand; thus it will act in the capacity of a herald of the impending event.[39]

If it is accepted as a strict chronology, Doctrine and Covenants 88:91–98 provides a nine-point sequence for how the events of the Second Coming will unfold.

1. During the period of natural calamities or "commotion," angels from heaven will tell earth's inhabitants to go out and meet the Bridegroom and prepare for the judgment of God.

2. The "great sign" will then be seen in heaven "immediately" or instantly.

3. An angel will then sound a trumpet and announce that the great and abominable church is ready to be burned.

4. There will be silence in heaven for half an hour.

5. Immediately thereafter the curtain of heaven will be unfolded, revealing the face of the Lord.

6. Another angel will then sound his trumpet. This will be the first trumpet in a series of seven.

7. The Saints who are alive on the earth will be "quickened" and caught up to meet the Savior.

8. The resurrection of celestial individuals will also take place, and these immortal beings will be caught up to meet Christ in the pillar of heaven.

9. The Saints who are caught up and the resurrected celestial individuals will finally descend with Christ to the earth.

Several comments in other scriptural texts or from LDS Church leaders provide a more detailed understanding of the sequence of events listed above.

1. Angels Will Appear During Natural Calamities

The Book of Mormon offers an instructive parallel to the appearance of angels who bear a heavenly message. Alma 13 relates that before the coming of Christ to the Nephites, angels declared unto the Lord's people in all nations that the day of salvation was drawing nigh and it was therefore expedient that they repent. This heaven-sent message was delivered "for the purpose of preparing the hearts of the children of men to receive [the Lord's] word at the time of His coming in His glory." The actual declaration that the Lord had arrived on the earth was expected to be delivered "unto just and holy men, by the mouth of angels, at the time of His coming," in order that prophecy might be fulfilled (Alma 13:21–26; cf. Mosiah 3:1–10). The appearance of angels to announce the coming of Christ is, of course, also found in the New Testament, which recounts that "a multitude of the heavenly host" participated in this activity (Luke 2:8–15).

2. The Great Sign Will Be Seen Immediately

The purpose behind the bright heavenly light known as the sign of the Son of Man appears to be that it will leave no doubt in the minds of mortals regarding the identity of the true Messiah. In the meridian of time, when the Lord spoke to His followers concerning His Second Advent, He said, "If they shall say unto you, Behold, he is in the desert; go not forth: Behold, he is in the secret chambers; believe it not; For as the light of the morning cometh out of the east, and shineth even unto the west, and covereth the whole earth, so shall also the coming of the Son of Man be" (JST, Matt. 24:26–27). The point of this scripture is simply that "if any man shall say unto you, Lo, here is Christ, or there; believe him not" (v. 21). "All flesh [will see] Him together" when He comes (D&C 101:23). There will be no doubt in anyone's mind about who the real Messiah is; His sign will act as one method of authentication.

3. An Angel Will Sound a Trumpet

In Doctrine and Covenants 29, the Lord states unequivocally that in accord with the prophecies of Ezekiel "the great and abominable church, which is the whore of all the earth, shall be cast down by devouring fire . . . for abominations shall not reign" (v. 21; cf. Ezek. 38:22). This is the most likely meaning of the phrase "the desolation of abomination in the last days," found in Doctrine and Covenants 84:117. Later in the same volume of scripture, it is referred to as "the desolation of abomination which awaits the wicked, both in this world and in the world to come," brought about by "the wrath of God" (D&C 88:85). Tribulation and desolation are slated to be "sent forth upon the wicked," says modern holy writ (D&C 29:8; cf. 63:37). Nevertheless, it must be remembered that the "day of desolation" and vengeance will begin with those members of the Church who are hypocrites to their avowed beliefs (see D&C 112:24–26).

4. Silence in Heaven

Regarding the half hour of silence in heaven—referred to both in Revelation 8:1 and Doctrine and Covenants 88:95—Elder Orson Pratt acknowledges that "whether the half hour . . . spoken of is according to our reckoning—thirty minutes, or whether it be according to the reckoning of the Lord we do not know. We know that the word 'hour' is used in some portions of the scriptures to represent quite a lengthy period of time. . . . [F]or [all] we know the half hour during which silence is to prevail in heaven may be quite an extensive period of time."[40] Based on the texts in Abraham 3:4 and in 2 Peter 3:8, it appears that the calculation of the ratio of the Lord's time to earth time is as follows:[41]

Lord's Time	Earth Time
1 day	1,000 years
1 hour	41.67 years
1 minute	253 days
1 second	4.22 days
0.25 second	1.1 days
0.01 second	1 hour

Thus, a half hour for the Lord would equal approximately twenty-one earth years. It is possible, therefore, that an appreciable period of time will pass between the opening of the seventh seal and certain signs of destruction prophesied to take place on the earth.[42]

5. The Curtain of Heaven Unfolded

Interesting terminology is used in Doctrine and Covenants 38:8 to describe the curtain of heaven to be parted at the Second Coming. Called a "veil of darkness," this peculiar designation implies that the partition conceals something that exhibits light. Doctrine and Covenants 88:95 denotes that it is "the face of the Lord" that is to be "unveiled" at the Second Coming, and passages from the Book of Mormon and New Testament verify that the face of the Redeemer shines with a visible light or glory (see 3 Ne. 19:24–25; Matt. 17:1–2).

6. Another Angel Sounds a Trumpet

As revealed in Doctrine and Covenants 29:26, it is Michael the archangel who will sound the resurrection trumpet. In this same collection of latter-day revelations, Michael is identified as Adam—the first man (D&C 107:54). Why would Adam (or Michael) be the one designated to inaugurate the redemption of the dead from their graves? One reason may be purely symbolic: Adam introduced death into the world (see 1 Cor. 15:21–22), so it seems appropriate that he play a role in the reversal of this condition. Another reason, as noted in Doctrine and Covenants 78:16, is that Deity has "given unto him the keys of salvation under the counsel and direction of the Holy One," or Jesus Christ.

7. The Saints "Quickened"

Elder Orson Pratt believed that at the Second Coming the mortal Saints will be "instantaneously caught up to meet the Lord in the air,"[43] and that they will be "renewed in a measure,"[44] "quickened . . . transfigured and sanctified, but not immortalized. They will be prepared for the millennial reign."[45] Elder Pratt elaborated upon this idea of a "partial change" by citing a similar occurrence when the Three Nephites were granted the same blessing as John the Revelator—to remain on the earth in an altered state of mortality without tasting death. In addition, they were to have neither physical pain nor sickness, nor sorrow for themselves. They could not be harmed, and Satan could have no power over them to tempt them. Then, at some future point, they would undergo, in the twinkling of an eye, a change to a completely immortal state. For this blessing to be granted, "the heavens were opened, and they were caught up into heaven," after which they were returned to the earth in a "sanctified" and "holy" state.[46] But what will happen to the other inhabitants of the earth who are not Saints but who are accounted worthy to live upon the earth during the millennial era? In the words of President Joseph Fielding Smith, "the inhabitants of the earth will have a sort of translation. They will be transferred to a condition of the terrestrial order, and so they will have power over disease and they will have power to live until they get a certain age and then they will die."[47]

8. Resurrection of Celestial Individuals

The resurrection of those who qualify for celestial glory began at the time of Christ's resurrection in Jerusalem (see Matt. 27:52–53) and will recommence when the Lord comes again—before the wicked are "cut off" from the earth (see D&C 45:45). The inheritors of celestial bodies will be individuals who have kept God's commandments and received His ordinances so that they can be "cleansed from *all* their sins" and thus be in a ritual condition that enables them to dwell eternally with holy beings (D&C 76:51–70; emphasis added). The "pillar of heaven" into which resurrected celestial personages will be caught up when Christ comes (D&C 88:97) is undoubtedly the same as the "pillar of fire" in which

Christ will arrive "at the day of [His] coming" (D&C 29:12). In the Old Testament, "the pillar of fire and of the cloud" was a visible symbol of the Lord's presence (Ex. 14:24; cf. Num. 14:14; Neh. 9:12, 19). When the Lord speaks in the Doctrine and Covenants about coming to earth "in a cloud with power and great glory," the imagery and symbolism are probably the same (D&C 34:7; cf. 45:44).

9. The Lord and His Saints Descend to Earth

When Jesus Christ ascended into heaven and was received by a cloud after His earthly ministry was complete, two angels testified that He would return someday "in like manner" (Acts 1:9–11). However, when He comes again, numerous angels will accompany Him to the earth in the clouds of heaven. The Lord's entourage will consist of "all the hosts" of heaven (D&C 29:11), otherwise identified as "all the holy angels" (D&C 45:44). Among this vast throng will be the Twelve Apostles who served with the Lord at Jerusalem (see D&C 29:12), the entire city of Enoch (see Moses 7:62–63), Adam, the prophet Moroni, Elias, Peter, James, John the Revelator, Elijah, Abraham, Isaac, Jacob, Joseph of Egypt, and John the Baptist (see D&C 27:5–12). Doctrine and Covenants 76 declares that the personages who descend with the Lord will do so in order to "reign on the earth over His people" (D&C 76:63; 43:29). They will have both the ability and authority to do so because they will have been made "kings" (D&C 76:56; cf. Rev. 5:10).

The Burning of the Wicked

One of the most vivid and frightening aspects of the Second Coming is the destruction of the wicked by fire when the Lord presents Himself to the entire world. Their destruction is assured because, as noted in canonized texts, no sinful or carnal person can see the Lord's face and live (see JST, Ex. 33:20; D&C 67:11–12).

The Lord has warned the Saints and also the inhabitants of the earth to "prepare . . . for the hour of judgment which is to come"

(D&C 88:84, 92). He also specifies that the judgment will come "upon all the nations that forget God, and upon all the ungodly among" His disciples (D&C 133:2).[48] Two separate revelations in the Doctrine and Covenants draw upon the imagery of Isaiah 34:5 to describe this judgment. They say that "the Lord . . . shall come down in judgment upon Idumea, or the world" (D&C 1:36) and "the Lord . . . shall come down upon the world with a curse to judgment" (D&C 133:2). In the text of Isaiah 34, "curse" is translated from the Hebrew word *herem,* which can also be rendered as "utter destruction."[49] This definition presents a graphic illustration of what will result from the judgment that is to come. Elder Bruce R. McConkie explains the term "Idumea" as follows: "Idumea or Edom, of which Bozrah was the principal city, was a nation to the south of the Salt Sea, through which the trade route (called the King's Highway) ran between Egypt and Arabia. The Idumeans or Edomites were a wicked non-Israelitish people; hence, traveling through their country symbolized to the prophetic mind the pilgrimage of men through a wicked world; and so Idumea meant the world."[50]

The terms "Edom" and "Bozrah" appear in an Old Testament text directly connected to the judgment that is to be carried out during the Second Coming. In this passage, Jehovah is pictured as coming from Edom and Bozrah wearing red apparel. The Lord explains the color of His clothing by declaring that in the day of vengeance He had trodden down the people in His indignation or wrath. His red robe symbolizes this act (Isa. 63:1–6). This text was modified by the Lord Jesus Christ in latter-day scripture.

> And it shall be said: Who is this that cometh down from God in heaven with dyed garments; yea, from the regions which are not known, clothed in His glorious apparel, traveling in the greatness of His strength?
>
> And He shall say: I am He who spake in righteousness, mighty to save.

> And the Lord shall be red in His apparel, and His garments like him that treadeth in the wine-vat.
> . . .
> And His voice shall be heard: I have trodden the wine-press alone, and have brought judgment upon all people; and none were with me;
> And I have trampled them in my fury, and I did tread upon them in mine anger, and their blood have I sprinkled upon my garments, and stained all my raiment; for this was the day of vengeance which was in my heart. (D&C 133:46–48, 50–51)

This will be a fateful "day of vengeance and burning" (D&C 85:3). Fire, long recognized as a cleansing agent, will be the means by which the earth is purified. The Lord promises that "the day cometh that the earth . . . shall be cleansed with fire" (JST, Heb. 6:7), and He reveals that it will be "at [His] command [that] the inhabitants thereof shall pass away, even so as by fire" (Ether 4:9).

A symbolic representation of the burning can be found in the parable of the wheat and the tares. In the New Testament, the Lord compares the world to a field, with the Son of Man represented as sowing "good seed" or wheat ("the children of the kingdom") in the field. The enemy (the devil) is represented as sowing "tares" ("the children of the wicked one") in the field. The "reapers" are the angels, and harvest time is pinpointed as "the end of the world." The text then given explains,"As therefore the tares are gathered and burned in the fire; so shall it be in the end of this world. The Son of Man shall send forth His angels, and they shall gather out of His kingdom all things that offend, and them which do iniquity; And shall cast them into a furnace of fire" (Matt. 13:40–42).

The Lord refers to this parable in revelations found in the Doctrine and Covenants. These texts note that the tares must be removed from the field so that they will not choke out the wheat.

Nevertheless, the two plants are allowed to grow together for a season until the wheat matures and becomes strong. Then the wheat is to be "secured in the garners," or a safe place, while the tares are to be bound in bundles with strong bands out in the field and "burned with unquenchable fire" (D&C 86:1–7; 101:63–66). The tares represent the great and abominable church that is to be "cast down by devouring fire" (D&C 88:94; 29:21). This symbolic church includes those who are "built up to get gain, and all those who are built up to get power over the flesh, and those who are built up to become popular in the eyes of the world, and those who seek the lusts of the flesh and the things of the world, and to do all manner of iniquity; yea, in fine, all those who belong to the kingdom of the devil." It is these people "who need fear, and tremble, and quake; they are those who must be brought low in the dust; they are those who must be consumed as stubble" (1 Ne. 22:23). In short, "all the proud and they that do wickedly shall be as stubble; and I will burn them up, saith the Lord of Hosts, that wickedness shall not be upon the earth" (D&C 29:9; cf. Malachi 4:1). But this group is not limited to human beings. Doctrine and Covenants 101 discloses that "every corruptible thing, both of man, or of the beasts of the field, or of the fowls of the heavens, or of the fish of the sea, that dwells upon all the face of the earth, shall be consumed" (v. 24–25).

Apparently, two different types of burning will occur. First, as stated in Doctrine and Covenants 5:19, the unrepentant will be "consumed away and utterly destroyed by the brightness of [Christ's] coming." Doctrine and Covenants 133:41, drawing upon the language of Isaiah 64:1–2, says that "the presence of the Lord shall be as the melting fire that burneth, and as the fire which causeth the waters to boil." The second type of burning will occur through angelic agency. A hint of this idea comes from the angel Moroni's rendition of Malachi 4:1. "Instead of quoting the first verse as [it] reads in our books," the Prophet Joseph Smith said, "he quoted it thus, 'For behold the day cometh that shall burn as an oven, and all the proud, yea, and all that do wickedly shall burn as stubble, for they that cometh shall burn them saith the Lord of hosts, that it shall leave them neither root nor branch.'"[51] Doctrine and Covenants section 63 is more informative. It refers to "the day of the coming of the Son of Man" and how at that time He will "send [His] angels to pluck out the wicked and cast them into unquenchable fire" (v. 53–54).

A few other insights on the fiery destruction of the wicked part of the world[52] can be gleaned by turning to the writings and words of authoritative sources.

According to articles published in the *Encyclopedia of Mormonism,* as well as numerous comments by LDS Church leaders, the earth has been baptized by water (when the wicked were destroyed in Noah's flood), and it will eventually be baptized by fire (when the wicked are destroyed at Christ's coming).[53] It appears that the earth is to imitate the stages of salvation required for human beings. The Book of Mormon teaches that "the baptism of fire and of the Holy Ghost" is the mechanism whereby individuals secure a "remission of . . . sins" (2 Ne. 31:14, 17). When Christ comes to the earth again, He will likewise remit or remove the sinful people of the planet by employing divine fire.

Of course, Latter-day Saints do not hold a monopoly on righteousness and will thus not be the only ones to survive the cleansing of the earth in the last days. On this topic, Elder James E. Talmage remarked:

> Now, many have asked, do we interpret . . . scripture as meaning that in the day of the Lord's coming, all who are not members of the Church shall be burned, or otherwise destroyed, and only this little body of men and women [called Latter-day Saints], very small compared with the uncounted hosts of men now living, shall be spared the burning and shall escape destruction? I think

> not so. I do not think we are justified in putting that interpretation upon the Lord's word, for He recognizes every man according to the integrity of his heart, and men who have not been able to understand the gospel or who have not had opportunity of learning it and knowing of it will not be counted as the willfully sinful who are fit only to be burned as stubble; but the proud, who lift themselves in the pride of their hearts and rise above the word of God and become a law unto themselves and who willfully and with knowledge deny the saving virtues of the Atonement of Christ, and who are seeking to lead others away from the truth will be dealt with by Him according to both justice and mercy.[54]

A final insight can be gained by considering the connection between the payment of tithing and protection from the Lord's burning. The doctrine that tithe-payers will not be burned at the Second Coming can be found in Doctrine and Covenants 64. It is sometimes overlooked that this blessing for obedience to divine law applies, as the Lord Himself has said, only to "[His] people" (v. 23). The law of tithing is designated in scripture as something that will "*prepare* [the Lord's people] against the day of vengeance and burning" (D&C 85:3; emphasis added). According to President Joseph F. Smith, the law of tithing determines who is loyal to the kingdom of God and who is against it. Tithe-payers demonstrate by action that their hearts are set on doing God's will—they are thus of a terrestrial (or spiritual) nature instead of a telestial (or worldly) nature, and will be allowed to remain on the earth when it becomes a terrestrial sphere.[55] Sometimes Saints lightheartedly assert that the payment of tithing is equivalent to fire insurance, and some may believe that the mere act of paying one's tithing is a guarantee of safety from the heaven-sent flame. But Elder Orson

Pratt taught that "'he that is tithed shall not be burned,' if he remain faithful in all things."[56]

The Second Coming of the Lord Jesus Christ will be both great and terrible. It will be terrible for those who choose not to turn from their wickedness, because they will be escorted from this sphere of existence amid the flames of the Lord's righteous indignation. But it will be a great day for those people who turn Satan from their hearts. Once the followers of the adversary are gone, the righteous will be prepared to embark on a golden age of happiness and peace.

Notes to Chapter 2

1. *WJS,* 8–9.

2. Ibid., 11.

3. Ibid., 10. "Daniel and John [the Revelator] each saw the opposition the little horn made against the Church of Jesus Christ of Latter-day Saints. This opposition will continue until the grand council is held at Adam-ondi-Ahman. This 'little horn' (Dan. 7:20–22; Rev. 13) is making a renewed and determined effort today to destroy the Church. The Lord has decreed otherwise and while its power will last until Michael comes and the Son of Man receives His rightful place, this great power will endure. It must, however, fall, and according to the scriptures its end will come rather suddenly (see D&C 29:21; 1 Ne. 13:1–9; Rev. chapters 17–18)" (Joseph Fielding Smith, *Church History and Modern Revelation* [Salt Lake City: The Council of the Twelve Apostles of The Church of Jesus Christ of Latter-day Saints, 1946–1949], 4:44; hereafter cited as *CHMR*).

4. *JD,* 18:336.

5. Joseph Fielding Smith, *The Way to Perfection* (Salt Lake City: Deseret Book, 1966), 290; hereafter cited as *WP.*

6. *CHMR,* 3:118.

7. *WJS,* 8–10. When Ezra Taft Benson was serving as a member of the Quorum of the Twelve Apostles, he indicated during a session of general conference that Adam would "meet with the leaders of his people" (CR, Oct. 1954, 119). Bruce R. McConkie agreed, stating that the Adam-ondi-Ahman event will be an appearance only "to selected members of [the Lord's] Church. He will come in private to His prophet and to the apostles then living" (*The Millennial Messiah,* 578–79).

8. *WJS,* 10.

9. *JD,* 18:330.

10. Ibid., 17:187.

11. Ibid., 18:343.

12. *WP,* 291. Bruce R. McConkie also states that the Lord's appearance at Adam-ondi-Ahman will be "secret" (*The Millennial Messiah,* 578–79).

13. *New Era,* December 1980, 49–50. President Brigham Young and Elder Orson Pratt both declared that the Lord will appear at New Jerusalem before He appears at Old Jerusalem (see *JD,* 11:279; 15:338). Elder Pratt is of the opinion that there will be "a long space of time" between these two visitations (ibid.).

14. *WJS,* 417.

15. *MFP,* 1:259.

16. *JD,* 15:365–66.

17. See ibid., 21:154.

18. *MS,* vol. 21, no. 37, 10 Sept. 1859, 582–83.

19. *WJS,* 242.

20. Ibid., 239.

21. Ibid., 233.

22. Ibid., 368.

23. CR, Oct. 1913, 98.

24. *WJS,* 318; emphasis added. An article published in 1918 represents the Salt Lake Temple recorder as saying, "John the Revelator, in the Apocalypse, refers to 144 thousand who are to appear on Mount Zion with the Redeemer, when He comes to reign on this earth. There could be no more effective way of entitling them to the distinction of association with the Savior than in serving as proxies for the dead, in the saving ordinances that are performed in God's holy temple. The prophet Obadiah said, 'Saviors shall come upon Mount Zion' [Obad. 1:21]" (Duncan M. McAllister, "Temple Ceremonies," *Improvement Era,* vol. 21, no. 3, Jan. 1918, 211; hereafter cited as *IE*).

25. See *T&S,* vol. 6, no. 3, 15 Feb. 1845, 809.

26. See *JD,* 14:243; 18:292; 19:320.

27. See Bruce R. McConkie, *Mormon Doctrine,* 2d ed. (Salt Lake City: Bookcraft, 1966), 546; hereafter cited as *MD.* Elder McConkie refers to the temple ordinances that the 144,000

receive: "There will be those among [the Saints] who advance and progress until they become kings and priests (see Rev. 1:1–6; 5:1–14; 20:4–6). John [the Revelator] sees 144,000 of these kings and priests, 12,000 from each tribe, converted, baptized, endowed, married for eternity, and finally sealed up unto eternal life, having their calling and election made sure [see 2 Pet. 1:1–19]. . . . [T]hrough the ordinances of the Lord's house they are to become kings and priests, who shall administer the blessings of the everlasting gospel to the Lord's elect (D&C 77:9–11)" (Bruce R. McConkie, *Doctrinal New Testament Commentary* [Salt Lake City: Bookcraft, 1973], 3:491, 494; hereafter cited as *DNTC*).

28. See Daniel H. Ludlow, ed., *Encyclopedia of Mormonism* (New York: Macmillan, 1992), 1:276, 2:479, 4:1766; hereafter cited as *EM;* Robert J. Matthews, *Selected Writings of Robert J. Matthews* (Salt Lake City: Deseret Book, 1999), 413; Joseph Fielding Smith, *Doctrines of Salvation* (Salt Lake City: Bookcraft, 1955), 2:41–42; hereafter cited as *DS;* Joseph Fielding Smith, *Man: His Origin and Destiny* (Salt Lake City: Deseret Book, 1954), 272; *WP,* 208; Bruce R. McConkie, *The Promised Messiah* (Salt Lake City: Deseret Book, 1978), 47; *NWAF,* 337; *MD,* 139–40, 546; *DNTC,* 3:230; *The Millennial Messiah,* 583, 700, 708. A patriarchal blessing given by John Smith in November 1845 to Joan Campbell tied together the 144,000 with the doctrines of exaltation. In this blessing Sister Campbell was told that she would "stand on Mount Zion with the 144,000 and enjoy all the blessings of eternal lives" (Robert L. Campbell journal, 20 Nov. 1845, cited in *Brigham Young University Studies,* vol. 29, no. 3, Summer 1989, 17).

29. Richard D. Draper, *Opening the Seven Seals: The Visions of John the Revelator* (Salt Lake City: Deseret Book, 1991), 83; hereafter cited as *OSS.*

30. *HC* 5:140.

31. See *WJS,* 170.

32. *HC* 4:493.

33. Ibid., 6:196.

34. *IE,* vol. 26, no. 11, Sept. 1923, 988.

35. Parley P. Pratt, *A Voice of Warning and Instruction to All People* (Salt Lake City: Deseret News Press, 1874), 49.

36. LeGrand Richards, *Israel! Do You Know?* (Salt Lake City: Deseret Book, 1954), 197.

37. *DNTC,* 3:509. See similar comments in *The Millennial Messiah,* 390.

38. *JD,* 8:49.

39. See *WJS,* 180–81.

40. *JD,* 16:328.

41. This chart is taken from Gerald N. Lund, *Selected Writings of Gerald N. Lund: Gospel Scholars Series* (Salt Lake City: Deseret Book, 1999), 260.

42. *The Millennial Messiah,* 382.

43. *JD,* 18:58.

44. Ibid., 19:176.

45. Ibid., 8:51–52.

46. Ibid., 16:320–22; 3 Ne. 28:1–30, 36–40.

47. Joseph Fielding Smith, *The Signs of the Times* (Independence, MO: Zion's Printing and Publishing Co., 1943), 39.

48. The destruction of the wicked within the Lord's Church is confirmed in these words: "The Son of Man shall send forth His angels, and they shall gather out of His kingdom all things that offend, and them which do iniquity; And shall cast them into a furnace of fire" (Matt. 13:41–42).

49. *SSECB,* 1391, Hebrew-Aramaic Dictionary, word #2764.

50. *MD,* 374.

51. *T&S,* vol. 3, no. 12, 15 Apr. 1842, 753; emphasis added.

52. "The world and earth are not synonymous terms. The world is the human family" (*WJS,* 60). "What is the end of the world? The destruction of the wicked" (ibid., 13; cf. JST, Matt. 24:4).

53. See *EM,* 3:1009, 1343; Elder John Taylor (*T&S,* vol. 5, no.

2, 15 Jan. 1844, 408); Brigham Young (*JD,* 8:83; 10:252; 17:117); Orson Pratt (ibid., 1:292, 331; 14:235; 16:318–19); Moses Thatcher (ibid., 26:309); Orson F. Whitney (ibid., 26:266; Brian H. Stuy, ed., *Collected Discourses* [Burbank, CA: B.H.S. Publishing, 1987], 1:167).

54. CR, Apr. 1916, 128.

55. See Joseph F. Smith, *Gospel Doctrine* (Salt Lake City: Deseret Book, 1986), 225. For further reading, see the discussion on "The Prophetic Type and Tithing," in Richard D. Rust, *Feasting on the Word: The Literary Testimony of the Book of Mormon* (Salt Lake City and Provo, UT: Deseret Book and The Foundation for Ancient Research and Mormon Studies, 1997), 212–14.

56. *MS,* vol. 6, no. 12, 1 Dec. 1845, 193; emphasis added.

CHAPTER 3

THE GREAT MILLENNIUM

The virtuous and just who have lived in previous dispensations of the gospel have sincerely hoped and earnestly prayed for a time when the works of darkness that pollute this world would be overthrown and abolished. They have dreamt of a day when Zion would be restored to the earth in all its fulness and glory (see Moses 7:62–63). They have eagerly anticipated a period when righteousness would reign supreme (see D&C 29:11; Rom. 5:21).

The Lord Jesus Christ has promised that in the future He will bring about these conditions. Near the beginning of the dispensation of the fulness of times, the Savior assured His latter-day disciples that "the great millennium, of which [He had] spoken by the mouth of [His] servants, [will] come" (D&C 43:30). This prospect gives mankind reason to rejoice, said James E. Talmage. Instead of the continual thought of the "lurid gloom" caused by actions that have enshrouded and "sickened" the nations of the earth for so long, the inhabitants of this planet can look to "the enlightening beams of comforting assurance that an era of peace is to be established. And this shall be a peace that cannot be broken, for righteousness shall rule, and man's birthright to liberty shall be inviolate."[1]

Parley P. Pratt provides a concise idea of what the Millennium entails and represents:

> The word *Millennium* signifies a thousand years, and in this sense of the word, may be applied to any thousand years, whether under the reign of wickedness or righteousness. But the term, *the Millennium,* is generally understood to apply to the particular thousand years which is mentioned in the scriptures as the reign of peace—the great Sabbath of creation, of which all other Sabbaths or jubilees seem to be but types. It is written, that "a thousand years is as one day, and one day as a thousand years, with the Lord" [2 Pet. 3:8; Abr. 3:4; Facsimile #2, fig. 1]. This being the case, then seven thousand years are seven days with the Lord, and the seventh or last thousand years, would, of course, be a Sabbath or jubilee; a rest, a grand release from servitude and woe.[2]

This explanation is comparable to a statement made by Joseph Smith that can be found in Doctrine and Covenants 77:12, where he refers to the fact that "on the seventh day [God] finished His work [of creation], and sanctified it. . . . [E]ven so," said the Prophet, "in the beginning of the seventh thousand years will the Lord God *sanctify* the earth" (emphasis added). This sanctification will bring about great changes; our planet will no longer suffer in its present tumultuous condition. As Jehovah informed the ancient prophet Enoch, "For the space of a thousand years the earth shall *rest*" (Moses 7:64; emphasis added).

Changes in the Earth, Animals, and Man

The canonized scriptures of the LDS Church and the commentary of its leaders include a number of statements that speak of changes that will eventually come upon the earth, the animals, and mankind during the millennial day.

Changes in the Earth

An interesting scriptural text concerning changes in the earth is Doctrine and Covenants 133:23–24. This passage relates how at some point in time Jesus Christ, the Creator of heaven and earth, will "command the great deep [or ocean], and it shall be driven back into the north countries, and the islands shall become one land; And the land of Jerusalem and the land of Zion shall be turned back into their own place, and the earth shall be like as it was in the days before it was divided." Thus, by the power of the Word the overall structure of the earth will be returned to its primordial condition. President Joseph Fielding Smith offers commentary on this concept:

> Just when this great change shall come we do not know. If, however, the earth is to be restored as it was in the beginning, then all the land surface will again be in one place as it was before the days of Peleg, when this great division was accomplished [see Gen. 10:25]. Europe, Africa, and the islands of the sea including Australia, New Zealand, and other places in the Pacific must be brought back and joined together as they were in the beginning.[3]

In the tenth Article of Faith, and in public discourse, the Prophet Joseph Smith spoke of another change that will affect this sphere. He declared that during the Millennium the earth will be renewed and resume its "paradisaic glory"—meaning that it will "become as the garden of the Lord" or the Garden of Eden.[4] This is a theme referred to regularly in early LDS literature and even in the hymnals of the Church. John Taylor, for example, taught that when the earth resumes the form of paradise it will be "delivered from under the curse" that was pronounced upon it by Deity after the fall of Adam and Eve.[5] President Brigham Young observed that the earth will return to its "paradisiacal state" and be "sanctified from the effects of the Fall" after being "baptized" and "cleansed" in Noah's flood and then "purified by fire" at the Second Coming.[6] Elder William E. McLellin wrote that the "peace . . . [of] the garden of Eden [will] be restored to the earth . . . for a thousand years."[7] It will be "the same earth in a different aspect," taught Elder Parley P. Pratt. The earth will be "renovated" and "renewed"; "conformed to the state of man, whose residence it is to be when man is redeemed."[8]

The idea that the earth will literally become verdant like the Garden of Eden is typically supported by LDS commentators who refer to prophecies recorded in the book of Isaiah. The prophet Isaiah points forward to a era when the desert will blossom abundantly and display "the glory of the Lord" and the "excellency" of God (Isa. 35:1–2). The Hebrew word translated as "excellency" in the King James Version of this passage is *hadar,* meaning "splendor" or "glory." This word can also be translated as "beauty."[9] Isaiah also states that the parched ground will become springs and pools of water, complete with aquatic life and vegetation (Isa. 35:5–6). In yet another portion of his writings, this Old Testament prophet makes it known that there will be a future reversal in the present order of nature that can be tied directly to the Garden of Eden. In that scripture he explains that myrtle trees and fir trees will grow where once grew "the thorn . . . [and] the brier" (Isa. 55:13). The connection to the world of primordial creation is located in Genesis 3:18, where it is said that when God cursed the earth after the fall of Adam and Eve, He caused it to produce thorns and thistles. The final example from Isaiah relating to future Edenic conditions on the earth states: "For the Lord shall comfort Zion: He will comfort all her waste places; and He will make her wilderness like Eden, and her desert like the garden of the Lord" (Isa. 51:3).[10]

Changes in the Animals

The idyllic conditions associated with the Adamic paradise will not be restricted to the millennial earth, however. Jesus Christ has indicated in modern revelation that during His thousand-year reign "the enmity of beasts . . . shall cease from before [His] face" (D&C 101:26). Elder Parley P. Pratt cites Isaiah 11:6, 10, as evidence that "so radical will be the change that voracious animals will feed on grass and not on flesh; venomous reptiles [will] become harmless playthings of children; beasts that are now antagonists [will] lie down together, and a general pacification [will] take place and prevail among all created beings [cf. Isa. 65:25]."[11] James E. Talmage ties together this lack of enmity to a concept in the book of Genesis. When Adam was in the Garden of Eden, notes Elder Talmage, he was "given dominion over the earth and its creatures" (see Gen. 1:26). During the Sabbatical era of the Millennium, mankind will be placed under Edenic conditions once again, and since men will be "relieved from the tyranny of Satan" during that time, they will be able to "rule by love." This will play an important role in the lessening of enmity between man and beast.[12] Another and undoubtedly connected factor that will figure prominently in the reduction of enmity in the animal kingdom is the Spirit of God. Brigham H. Roberts pointed to the prophecy of Joel 2:28 and taught that "its complete fulfillment, requires that the Spirit of the Lord, the Holy Ghost, shall be poured out upon *all flesh.*" This situation, said Elder Roberts, "undoubtedly refers to that time which shall come in the blessed millennium when the enmity . . . between the beasts of the forests and of the fields; and between man and beast, as described by Isaiah" shall cease.[13]

Changes in Man

In addition to changes in the earth and the animals when the Lord reigns, there will be distinct alterations in the constitution of mankind. These changes are listed by the Lord in Doctrine and Covenants 101.

No More Enmity. The first item on this list that draws attention is that "the enmity of man . . . shall cease" (D&C 101:26). In one of the prophecies found in the book of Joel, which speaks of the battle of Armageddon, the Lord talks of preparation for this "war" by employing the following imagery: "Beat your *plowshares into swords,* and your *pruninghooks into spears*" (3:9–14; emphasis added). However, the prophecies of Isaiah concerning what will "come to pass in the last days" indicate that this situation will be reversed. In the millennial day, men "shall beat their *swords into plowshares,* and *their spears into pruninghooks:* nation shall not lift up sword against nation, neither shall they learn war anymore" (Isa. 2:4; emphasis added). An obvious cause-and-effect principle is involved in this future event. The prophecies of Joel and the writings of the Apostle Paul provide further insight into this change of heart. In Joel's prophecies the Lord foretells the time when the Spirit will be poured out upon all flesh (see Joel 2:28), and Paul explains that the fruits of, or things that are produced by, the Spirit of God include gentleness, love, and peace (see Gal. 5:22). Thus, the presence of the Spirit among all the peoples of the earth will remove the desire for war and other types of conflict. Inasmuch as chaotic forces and behavior originate with Satan (see Moses 6:15), when power is taken away from him at the time of the Second Coming, the consequence will be a thousand years of peace.

Heightened Religious Experience. The next change in store for mankind relates to interaction with Deity. "In that day," proclaims the Lord in Doctrine and Covenants 101:27, "whatsoever any man shall ask, it shall be given unto him." In a parallel passage of scripture, the Lord says, "And it shall come to pass, that before they call, I will answer; and while they are yet speaking, I will hear" (Isa. 65:24). Again, this situation can be tied directly to the prophetic book of Joel, where the Lord states that He will pour out His Spirit upon all flesh (see Joel 2:28). This is significant because in the law associated with prayer found in the Doctrine and Covenants, the Lord stipulates that "he that asketh in Spirit shall receive in Spirit . . . [because] He that asketh in the Spirit *asketh according to the will of God;* wherefore it is done even as he asketh. And again, I say unto you, all things must be done in the name of Christ, whatsoever you do in the Spirit" (D&C 46:28, 30–31; emphasis added). And in another section of modern-day canon the Master adds the qualification that *"if ye are purified and cleansed from all sin,* ye shall ask whatsoever you will in the name of Jesus and *it shall be done"* (D&C 50:29–30; emphasis added). These scriptural texts lead to the conclusion that during the Millennium there will be times when the Lord will reveal through the Spirit which blessings He is willing to grant to certain qualified individuals, and through prayer, in the name of the Son of God, these blessings will be given. These prayers, therefore, can be understood as prophecies that are certain to be fulfilled.

An additional scripture points toward another type of millennial interaction with the Lord. In Doctrine and Covenants 84, the Lord speaks of the post-scourge era, saying that in progression of time, "all shall know [Him], who remain, even from the least unto the greatest" (v. 98). This scripture has clear allusions to Jeremiah 31:34, where the God of the Old Testament declares, "And they shall teach no more every man his neighbour, and every man his brother, saying, Know the Lord: for they shall all know me, from the least of them unto the greatest of them, saith the Lord." The Prophet Joseph Smith taught that these particular references about knowing the Lord are connected with making one's calling and election sure (in association with the sealing power) and the reception of the Second Comforter, which is a personal visitation from the Redeemer Himself, who will teach the individual who receives this sacred privilege the mysteries of His kingdom.[14]

The Binding of Satan. Another blessing that the peoples of the earth will enjoy during the millennial age is that "in that day Satan shall not have power to tempt any man" (D&C 101:28). The enemy of all righteousness will be unable to draw away mankind because he will be "bound, that he shall have no place in the hearts of the children of men" (D&C 45:55). This binding will last for the space of one thousand years (see D&C 88:110). John the Revelator saw in vision that an angel from heaven will bind Satan with a great chain and cast him into a bottomless pit. The sealing of the pit will prevent the adversary from deceiving the nations of the earth any further (see Rev. 20:1–3). In April 1900, President Joseph F. Smith spoke about the binding of the wicked one: "As to whether the binding of Satan is a literal binding as with a chain or not, it matters not. I am inclined to believe that the chain spoken of in the Bible, with which Satan is to be bound, is more figurative than real. He will be bound both by the faith of the righteous and the decrees of the Almighty during the millennial reign and will be cast down into hell, as the prophets have said, and shall not be at liberty to molest the children of men until the end of the thousand years."[15]

Even if the chain that constrains Satan in the book of Revelation is seen merely as a symbol, it must still be acknowledged that the binding is being accomplished by the power of heaven—since an angel of God carries out the act. Joseph Fielding Smith notes that "there are many among us who teach that the binding of Satan will be merely the binding which those dwelling on the earth will place upon him by their refusal to hear his enticings. This is not so," insists President Smith, since the arch-enemy of all that is good "will not have the *privilege* during that period of time to tempt any man."[16]

Just because Satan will be bound during the millennial reign of the King of Kings, it does not follow that all mortals on the earth during that reign will be accounted as righteous. On March 16, 1841, the Prophet Joseph Smith asserted that "the wicked will not all be destroyed at the coming of Christ and also there will be wicked [people] during the millennium."[17] On December 30, 1842, the Prophet made a similar comment: "There will be wicked men on the earth during the thousand years."[18] This concept is confirmed in Doctrine and Covenants 76, where the Prophet relates that people who can abide a terrestrial kingdom include those who are "honorable men of the earth" but who, when they have the gospel of the Son of God preached unto them "while in the flesh," choose not to receive "the testimony of Jesus" (v.

71–75). The Lord describes those who do not receive His voice and come unto Him as being "under darkness," "under the bondage of sin," and "wicked" (D&C 84:49–53). These two scriptures thus lead to the conclusion that the Lord will consider those who live on the millennial (or terrestrial) earth, but who choose to reject His gospel, as being wicked individuals.[19]

This finding leads to a related question. Orson Pratt asked, "Will it be possible for men to sin during the millennium?" He answered:

> Yes. Why? Because they have not lost their agency. Agency always continues wherever intelligent beings are, whether in heaven, on the earth, or among any of the creations that God has made; wherever you find intelligent beings, there you will find an agency. Not to the same extent, perhaps, under all circumstances but yet there is always the exercise of agency where there is intelligence. For instance, when Satan is bound and a seal set upon him in [the] lowermost pit, his agency [will be] partially destroyed in some things. He will not have power to come out of that pit; now he has that power. Then he will not have power to tempt the children of men; now he has that power. Consequently his agency then will be measurably destroyed or taken away, but not in full. The Lord will not destroy the agency of the people during the millennium, therefore there will be a possibility of their sinning during that time. But if they who live then do sin, it will not be because of the power of the devil to tempt them, for he will have no power over them. . . . [T]hey will sin merely because they choose to do so of their own free will.[20]

In the book of Isaiah, Jehovah verifies that during the Millennium a person can be classified as a "sinner," and He reveals that such a person will be "accursed" (Isa. 65:20). Elder Bruce R. McConkie, in referring directly to this scripture, says, "Isaiah's description of life and death during the millennium seems to preserve the concept that even then—even in that blessed day when Satan is bound and righteousness overflows—even then men are free to come out in open rebellion and, as sinners, suffer the fate reserved for the sons of perdition. Manifestly, they, being accursed, would die the death with which we are familiar, for their resurrection is destined to be in that final day when those [people] shall come forth who shall 'remain filthy still' (D&C 88:102)."[21] In addition, those who are living in the terrestrial condition of the Millennium but who choose to live on a telestial level will also die physically and will have to await the end of the thousand-year reign of Christ before they have the opportunity to be resurrected (see D&C 88:101).

Length and Type of Mortality. Another change slated for man during the millennial day is a different length and type of mortality. Death came upon human beings when Adam fell from his terrestrial state in the Garden of Eden (see Moses 6:48). When the earth is returned to its Edenic condition, mankind will be restored to a mode of life where death does not hold sway. The Savior announces, in Doctrine and Covenants 101, that during the time when His kingdom is triumphant "there shall be no sorrow because there is no death. In that day," He says, "an infant shall not die until he is old; and his life shall be as the age of a tree; And when he dies he shall not sleep, that is to say in the earth, but shall be changed in the twinkling of an eye, and shall be caught up, and his rest shall be glorious" (v. 29–31; cf. Isa. 65:19–20). Likewise, even though those people who are alive after Christ's return are considered to be in a "blessed" state, it is nevertheless "appointed to [them] to die at the age of man. Wherefore, children shall grow up until they become old; old men shall die; but they shall not sleep in the dust, but they shall be changed in the twinkling of an eye" (D&C 63:50–51). As noted above, not everyone will qualify for an instant resurrection at the point of millennial death. The celestial and terrestrial resurrections will be in progress near the beginning of the Millennium; thus those who have been judged worthy of either of these rewards will be transferred to a permanent, immortal condition quickly. However, those people deemed deserving of a resurrection of the telestial type or as a son of perdition will have to wait until the end of Christ's reign before they can arise from their graves.

Increased Knowledge. Another blessing that is poured out upon men and women during the millennial age of the earth will be a marvelous increase in knowledge. Orson Pratt teaches that during this time mankind will become the recipient of profuse counsel, instruction, and revelation from the Redeemer.

> Do you suppose that [Jesus Christ] will give no new revelation during that time, but that He will sit on His throne like the idols in some of the heathen nations? Do you suppose that the Lord Jesus, that intelligent Being, by whom the Father made the worlds, is coming here to reign King of kings, and to sit down on His throne in the temple at Jerusalem, and upon His throne in His temple in Zion, and abide there as a statue from generation to generation, for a thousand years, and when the people come up to ask Him a question that He will not say a word, only to tell them they have enough? Do you suppose this will be the case? Oh no, my friends, the Lord Jesus will converse the whole thousand years with His people, and give them instruction. He will reign over the house of David, over the children of Israel, over the twelve tribes, over Zion and over all the inhabitants of the

> earth (that is, over all who are spared in that day) giving counsel here, instructions yonder, revealing something there, and so on, and the amount of revelation that will be given during the thousand years will no doubt be ten thousand times more than is contained in [the] Bible.[22]

Indeed, the Savior promises in Doctrine and Covenants 101 that "in that day when the Lord shall come, He shall reveal all things" (v. 32; see also v. 25). A prototype of this outpouring of knowledge can be seen in the visit of Jesus Christ to the Nephites after His Resurrection. At that time, He expounded on all things from the beginning and through the day of judgment (see 3 Ne. 26:1–6). As Deity states in the book of Isaiah, "The earth shall be full of the knowledge of the Lord, as the waters cover the sea" (11:9; cf. D&C 84:98). The Prophet Joseph Smith interpreted this verse to mean that "the earth will be filled with sacred knowledge, as the waters cover the great deep."[23] The Lord's revelations offer a glimpse of what is to be revealed in that great day. The followers of the Son of Man will be instructed concerning "things which have passed, and hidden things which no man knew, things of the earth, by which it was made, and the purpose and the end thereof—Things most precious, things that are above, and things that are beneath, things that are in the earth, and upon the earth, and in heaven" (D&C 101:33–34).

Furthermore, says the Lord, mankind will be taught

> whether there be one God or many gods, they shall be manifest.
>
> All thrones and dominions, principalities and powers, shall be revealed and set forth upon all who have endured valiantly for the gospel of Jesus Christ.
>
> And also, if there be bounds set to the heavens or to the seas, or to the dry land, or to the sun, moon, or stars—

> All the times of their revolutions, all the appointed days, months, and years, and all the days of their days, months, and years, and all their glories, laws, and set times, shall be revealed in the days of the dispensation of the fulness of times. (D&C 121:28–31)

In fact, the Book of Mormon declares that "the things of all nations shall be made known; yea, all things shall be made known unto the children of men. There is nothing which is secret save it shall be revealed; there is no work of darkness save it shall be made manifest in the light; and there is nothing which is sealed upon the earth save it shall be loosed. Wherefore, all things which have been revealed unto the children of men shall at that day be revealed" (2 Ne. 30:16–18).

A Pure Language. One final insight into changes among men and women during the Millennium (which has yet another connection with the Garden of Eden) can be gleaned from the Old Testament. In Zephaniah 3:8–9, the Lord utters a prophecy that contains definite references to the last days. Jehovah speaks of His determination to gather the kingdoms or nations of the earth so that He can pour out His fierce anger and indignation upon them. He then says, "For all the earth shall be devoured with the fire of my jealousy." This set of verses clearly refers to the battle of Armageddon, the Second Coming, or both. Immediately after making these pronouncements, the Lord reveals, "For then will I turn to the people a pure language that they may all call upon the name of the Lord, to serve Him with one consent." In a Church article about the prophecy of Zephaniah, written in 1834, the author definitely expected the return of the pure language after the time when the wicked inhabitants of the earth are burned and removed from the mortal sphere.[24]

Matthias F. Cowley offers the following perspective regarding this portion of Zephaniah's writings. He reported that "The pure language was confounded at the tower of Babel because men sought to thwart the purposes of Jehovah. When the time comes that the wicked who will not obey are swept from the earth, the Lord will restore to His children the language which they learned from their mother tongue and which was spoken from Adam (cf. Moses 6:5–6) to the time of the tower of Babel" (cf. Gen. 11:5–8).[25]

In 1854, Wilford Woodruff recorded in his journal that he had passed a pleasant evening in company with Elizabeth A. Whitney and Eliza R. Snow. Before the two women left the place of meeting, wrote Elder Woodruff, "they sang in tongues in the pure language which Adam and Eve spoke in the Garden of Eden." This was not the first time that the language of paradise had been manifested among the Latter-day Saints. "This gift," related Elder Woodruff, "was obtained in the Kirtland Temple [in the mid-1830s] through a promise of the Prophet Joseph Smith. He told Sister Whitney if she would rise upon her feet she should have the pure language. She did so, and immediately began to sing in tongues." Elder Woodruff remembered, "It was nearer to heavenly music than anything I ever heard."[26]

"I make all things new," says the God of creation in a revelation about the future (Rev. 21:5). This saying will have profound meaning during the millennial day when the earth, animals, mankind, and life itself will be transformed—brought back to a higher order of things, re-created. With such conditions prevailing, the kingdom of God will be able not only to exist in its intended fulness on the earth, but will also have the means to flourish.

The Millennial Kingdom of God

Within the holy scriptures, both ancient and modern, can be found the concept of God establishing His heavenly kingdom upon the face of the earth. This is the only earthly empire that is destined to exist and grow for eternity.

In an inspired dream, the prophet Daniel learned that before the time when the Ancient of Days (or Adam) meets with the Son of Man (or Jesus Christ), a kingly power will arise and make war with the Saints and prevail against them. But then Daniel saw that "thrones [will be] cast down," "dominion" will be "taken away" from earthly kings, and an especially terrible and destructive king—who is the enemy of the Saints—will be "destroyed, and given to the burning flame." The ancient Israelite prophet was also shown that the Son of Man will be given "an everlasting dominion" and a kingdom that will never be destroyed. Daniel was further informed that "the Saints of the Most High [will] take the kingdom, and possess the kingdom forever," and "judgment" will be given unto them (Dan. 7:2–27).

Similarly, in the Apostle John's grand prophetic vision of the future known as the book of Revelation, he understood that after the death and resurrection of the two prophets in Jerusalem at the battle of Armageddon, and the subsequent destruction of the enemies of Israel, there will be an announcement made in heaven proclaiming, "The kingdoms of this world are become the kingdom of our Lord, and of His Christ; and He shall reign forever and ever." The meridian Apostle was also shown something that may seem to be somewhat enigmatic at first: the ark of the covenant in the heavenly temple (JST, Rev. 11:3–19). This display of an Israelite temple symbol makes perfect sense when it is understood that the ark—kept in the Holy of Holies of the Lord's house—represents God's throne.[27] Thus, the announcement heard by John of never-ending dominion is accompanied by the presentation of a symbol that was anciently understood to represent the Lord's kingship.

Revelations found in the Doctrine and Covenants frequently mention the latter-day kingdom of God. For instance, "the kingdom" is equated with "the keys of the Church" in Doctrine and Covenants 42:69. In section 105 of that same volume, the Lord confirms to Latter-day Saints—in language correlating with that which was heard by the Apostle John—that eventually "the kingdoms of this world" will be "constrained to acknowledge that the kingdom of Zion is in very deed the kingdom of our God and His Christ" (v. 32). And in section 65 the Lord verifies that "the kingdom of God . . . is [now] set up on the earth" and "the keys of the kingdom of God are committed unto man on the earth." At the instigation of this kingdom, says the Lord, "the gospel [will] roll forth unto the ends of the earth, as the stone which is cut out of the mountain without hands shall roll forth, until it has filled the whole earth" (v. 2, 5–6; cf. 109:72). This language directly parallels the prophetic dream interpreted by Daniel (see Dan. 2:34–35, 44–45).

While Sidney Rigdon was serving as a counselor in the First Presidency of the LDS Church in 1834, he wrote that the abolishment of the kingdoms of the earth will not be a figurative occurrence, but rather a literal one. He teaches that Jesus Christ

> will as literally break in pieces and destroy all the kingdoms of the world, as ever one king destroyed and broke down the kingdom of another. Never did Cyrus the Great, more literally break down and destroy the kingdom of ancient Babylon, than will Christ, the Great King break in pieces and destroy all the kingdoms of the world; and so completely will He do it, that there will not from one end of the earth to another be an individual found whose word or edict will be obeyed but His own: so that He will completely break in pieces and destroy all kingdoms.[28]

The Lord has manifested in a latter-day revelatory text that it is His "right" to reign as King over the inhabitants of the earth (D&C 58:22). Furthermore, His reign will be of a universal nature, for it has been declared by Him that it will be "over all flesh" (D&C 133:25; emphasis added). The Prophet Joseph Smith states that "it has been the design of Jehovah, from the commencement of the world, and is His purpose now, to regulate the affairs of the world in His own time; to stand as head of the universe, and take the reins of government into His own hand." Thus, His millennial government will be administered as a "theocracy."[29]

The Saints Will Reign

The nucleus for the millennial government of God has already been placed upon the earth—it is called The Church of Jesus Christ of Latter-day Saints. In regard to the future manifestation of the kingdom, James E. Talmage teaches that "the Church must be regarded as a part thereof; an essential [part] indeed, for it is the germ from which the kingdom is to be developed, and the very heart of the organization. The Church has existed and now continues in an organized form, without the kingdom as an established power with temporal authority in the world; but the kingdom cannot be maintained without the Church."[30]

A prophecy printed in the Doctrine and Covenants foretells that the members of God's earthly kingdom will play an active role in administering it. The Savior Himself revealed, "My people . . . shall reign with me on earth" (D&C 43:29; cf. 84:119; Rev. 5:10). In John the Revelator's vision, he "saw thrones, and [those who stood as witnesses for Jesus and the word of God] sat upon them, and judgment was given unto them . . . and they lived and reigned with Christ a thousand years" (Rev. 20:4). Elder Bruce R. McConkie, in referring to the tenth Article of Faith and explaining the concept of the reigning Saints, notes that "'Christ will reign personally upon the earth' . . . and with Him, in like glory, exercising rule and dominion, each in his appointed sphere, shall be all those who, through righteousness, have become kings and priests."[31] Elder McConkie clarifies this idea by noting that

> John [the Revelator] tells us that "Jesus Christ . . . hath made us [the faithful elders of His kingdom] kings and priests unto God and His Father" (Rev. 1:5–6). And we might add, He hath made the faithful sisters of His kingdom queens and priestesses. And further: He hath "made us unto our God kings and priests: and we shall reign on the earth" (Rev. 5:10). What is a king without a kingdom? Unless they are given dominion and power over an appointed kingdom, their reign will be shallow and powerless.
>
> If righteous men come up in the resurrection to reign as kings, and if Christ our Lord is their King, then He, as the scriptures say, is a King of kings. [See Rev. 17:14; 19:16][32]

Governmental Structure

The delegation of power to rule in the earthly kingdom of Jesus Christ will be necessary during the Millennium because He will not always be physically present on the earth. "Christ and the resurrected Saints will reign over the earth, but not dwell on the earth," said Joseph Smith. They will rather "visit it when they please or when [it is] necessary to govern it."[33] Likewise, the Prophet taught the following: "That Jesus will be a resident on the earth a thousand [years] with the Saints is not the case. But [He] will reign over the Saints and come down and instruct [them] as He did the five hundred brethren [after His resurrection (see 1 Cor. 15:6)]. And those of the first resurrection will also reign with Him over the Saints."[34]

It is important to understand, however, that not everyone who administers the kingdom of God on the earth during the Millennium will actually hold membership in the household of faith. George Q. Cannon taught this principle irrefutably.

> We have been taught from the beginning this important principle, that the Church of God is

> distinct from the kingdom of God. Joseph [Smith] gave us the pattern before he died. He gave his brethren an example that has not been forgotten up to this day. He impressed it upon them, that men, [who were] not members of the Church, could be members of the kingdom that the Lord will set up when He reigns. . . . In the minds of all of us who understand this matter there is a clear distinction between the Church in its ecclesiastical capacity and that which may be termed the government of God in its political capacity.[35]

The political entity President Cannon referred to was an organization sometimes called the Council of Fifty. The *Encyclopedia of Mormonism* defines this council as a group sanctioned by the Prophet during the Nauvoo era of Church history. It championed scriptural ethics and the responsibilities and protections of the United States Constitution, and its aim was to establish the seed of God's theocratic millennial kingdom in a pluralistic society. The First Presidency and Quorum of the Twelve Apostles belonged to the Council of Fifty (with the Church President in charge), but three of the members of the council were not members of the restored Church.[36] Joseph Fielding Smith emphasizes the significance of this mixture in the council:

> After Christ comes, all the peoples of the earth will be subject to Him, but there will be multitudes of people on the face of the earth who will not be members of the Church; yet all will have to be obedient to the laws of the kingdom of God, for it will have dominion upon the whole face of the earth. These people will be subject to the political government, even though they are not members of the ecclesiastical kingdom or [the restored Church of Jesus Christ].[37]

President Brigham Young adamantly taught that the existence of the millennial kingdom will not nullify any person's freedom of religion, declaring, "If the Latter-day Saints think, when the kingdom of God is established on the earth, that all the inhabitants of the earth will join the Church called Latter-day Saints, *they are egregiously mistaken.* I presume there will be as many sects and parties then as now."[38] On another occasion, President Young stated that

> When the kingdom of God is fully set up and established on the face of the earth, and takes the pre-eminence over all other nations and kingdoms, it will protect the people in the enjoyment of all their rights, no matter what they believe, what they profess, or what they worship. . . . [It] will sustain and uphold every individual in what they deem their individual rights, so far as they do not infringe upon the rights of their fellow creatures . . . [and] so far as their notions [are] not incompatible with the laws of the kingdom.[39]

Neal A. Maxwell does not seem to think that social diversity during the thousand-year reign of Christ will generate social disorder—as sometimes occurs in the present telestial world. He says, "We understand, of course, that there will be many nonmembers of the Church living during the Millennium, but there will be a clear willingness by all the good and decent men and women of all the races, creeds, and cultures to abide by a terrestrial law."[40]

Dual Capitals of the Kingdom

One final aspect of the millennial government of God should be mentioned—the location of the capital of the kingdom. Joseph

Fielding Smith, in an official Church publication, states: "There are to be two great capitals. One [in the] Jerusalem of old and the other [in] the City of Zion, or New Jerusalem. The latter is to be on this [American] continent. The one will be the Lord's headquarters for the people of Judah and Israel his companions; the other for Joseph and his companions on the Western Hemisphere, which was given to Joseph and his seed after him as an everlasting inheritance."[41] According to Elder Bruce R. McConkie, "the building of these two world capitals will commence before the second coming and continue during the millennium."[42] The book of scripture most often appealed to for support of this doctrine is Isaiah: "Out of Zion shall go forth the law, and the word of the Lord from Jerusalem" (Isa. 2:3); likewise, "the Lord of hosts shall reign in mount Zion, and in Jerusalem" (Isa. 24:23). This duality is also referred to in Doctrine and Covenants 133:21, where specific mention is made of the voice of the Lord being uttered from the two locations. In certain Book of Mormon texts, the Savior explains that at the New Jerusalem "the powers of heaven" will come down among the Lord's people and that He Himself will be "in the midst" of them (3 Ne. 20:22; 21:23–25). A parallel text in modern scripture clarifies that this will be connected with the administration of divine law: "For the Lord shall be in their midst, and His glory shall be upon them, and He will be their king and their lawgiver" (D&C 45:59). In referring to the situation at Old Jerusalem, the Prophet Joseph Smith explains that "then shall the law of the Lord go forth from Zion and the word of the Lord to the priests and through them from Jerusalem."[43] Orson F. Whitney proposes that we think of the dual capitals of Zion and Jerusalem from an interesting Old Testament perspective:

> David's ancient empire, which parted in twain, forming the kingdom of Judah and the kingdom of Israel, may it not have been a foreshadowing of God's greater empire of the last days, which will

> consist of two grand divisions—two in one? Here upon the Land of Zion, "a land choice above all other lands" [Ether 2:10], the children of Joseph, the descendants of Ephraim, are even now assembling to make preparation for Messiah's advent. The Jews will greet Him at Jerusalem. Christ's kingdom will have two capitals, one in the Old World, one in the New; one in America, the other in Palestine. "For out of Zion shall go forth the law, and the word of the Lord from Jerusalem" [Isa. 2:3].[44]

Regardless of which capital Latter-day Saints may find themselves associated with in the future, they have been instructed by the King of the entire empire to follow the example of Jesus Christ in praying to the Lord "that His kingdom may go forth upon the earth" and prosper, that when the Son of Man descends and unites with that kingdom God may be glorified on earth as He is in heaven (D&C 65:5–6; cf. Matt. 6:9–10).

Notes to Chapter 3

1. James E. Talmage, *The Vitality of Mormonism* (Boston: Gorham Press, 1919), 176; hereafter cited as *VM.*

2. *MS,* vol. 1, no. 1, May 1840, 7.

3. Joseph Fielding Smith, *Answers to Gospel Questions* (Salt Lake City: Deseret Book, 1966), 5:74; hereafter cited as *AGQ.*

4. *T&S,* vol. 3, no. 9, 1 Mar. 1842, 710; no. 18, 15 July 1842, 855.

5. Ibid., vol. 2, no. 13, 1 May 1841, 400.

6. *JD,* 17:117.

7. *MA,* vol. 1, no. 7, Apr. 1835, 103.

8. *MS,* vol. 6, no. 1, 15 June 1845, 10.

9. *SSECB,* 1380, Hebrew-Aramaic Dictionary, word #1926.

10. For commentary on passages from the book of Isaiah and the idea of Edenic renewal for the earth, see Craig J. Ostler, "Isaiah's Voice on the Promised Millennium," in *Voices of Old Testament Prophets* (Salt Lake City: Deseret Book, 1997), 72–73; Donald W. Parry, Jay A. Parry, and Tina M. Peterson, *Understanding Isaiah* (Salt Lake City: Deseret Book, 1998), 118–20.

11. *MS,* vol. 6, no. 1, 15 June 1845, 10.

12. *VM,* 177.

13. Brigham H. Roberts, *A Comprehensive History of The Church of Jesus Christ of Latter-day Saints* (Salt Lake City: Deseret News Press, 1930), 1:xxxix; emphasis in original; hereafter cited as *CHC.*

14. *WJS,* 4–5.

15. Hyrum M. Smith III and Scott G. Kenney, comp., *From Prophet to Son: Advice of Joseph F. Smith to His Missionary Sons* (Salt Lake City: Deseret Book, 1981), 71. For more references on Satan being bound, see D&C 43:31; 84:100; 1 Ne. 22:26; 2 Ne. 30:18.

16. *CHMR,* 1:175.

17. *WJS,* 65.

18. *HC* 5:212.

19. Joseph Fielding Smith advocated this line of logic in *WP,* 313. He specifically singled out the "heathen" and those who "have not come into the Church" as those who will reject the gospel and thus be classed among the wicked of the millennial era.

20. *JD,* 16:319–20.

21. *The Millennial Messiah,* 646.

22. *JD,* 15:110.

23. *HC* 2:357; emphasis added. President Lorenzo Snow taught that the Messiah will "explain the mysteries of the kingdom, and tell us things that are not lawful to talk about now" (CR, Apr. 1898, 14).

24. See *Evening and Morning Star,* vol. 2, no. 18, Mar. 1834, 142; hereafter cited as *EMS.*

25. Matthias F. Cowley, *Cowley's Talks on Doctrine* (Chattanooga, TN: Benjamin E. Rich, 1902), 186–87.

26. Mathias F. Cowley, comp., *Wilford Woodruff: History of His Life and Labors* (Salt Lake City: Bookcraft, 1964), 355. For further reading, see the entry on "Adamic Language" in *EM,* 1:18–19.

27. See Matthew B. Brown, *The Gate of Heaven: Insights on the Doctrines and Symbols of the Temple* (American Fork, UT: Covenant, 1999), 74–75, 86–87, 98–99.

28. *EMS,* vol. 2, no. 21, June 1834, 162.

29. *T&S,* vol. 3, no. 18, 15 July 1842, 856–57.

30. *SAF,* 366. Wilford Woodruff stated: "We believe this Church will prepare the way for the coming of Christ to reign as King, and that this Church will then develop into the kingdom of God" (*MS,* vol. 52, no. 11, 17 Mar. 1890, 162). Brigham Young disclosed that "that kingdom grows out of the Church of Jesus Christ of Latter-day Saints, but it is not the Church, for a man may be a legislator in that body which will issue laws to sustain the inhabitants of the earth in their individual rights and still not belong to the Church of Jesus Christ at all" (*JD,* 2:310).

31. *DNTC,* 3:573.

32. *The Millennial Messiah,* 640. Elder McConkie explained part of the process of becoming a "king" in God's kingdom: "Those who endure in perfect faith, who receive the Melchizedek Priesthood, and who gain the blessings of the temple (including celestial marriage) are eventually ordained *kings* and *priests.* These are offices given faithful holders of the Melchizedek Priesthood, and in them they will bear rule as exalted beings during the millennium and in eternity" (*MD,* 599; emphasis in original).

33. Scott H. Faulring, ed., *An American Prophet's Record: The Diaries and Journals of Joseph Smith* (Salt Lake City: Smith Research Associates, 1987), 262.

34. *WJS,* 65.

35. *CD,* 5:295–96.

36. See *EM,* 1:326–27.

37. *DS,* 1:229.

38. *JD,* 11:275; emphasis added.

39. Ibid., 2:309–10. President Young asked, "When the kingdom of heaven spreads over the whole earth, do you expect that all the people composing the different nations will become Latter-day Saints? If you do, you will be much mistaken. Do you expect that every person will be destroyed from the face of the earth, but the Latter-day Saints? If you do, you will be mistaken. . . . [T]he order of society will be as it is when Christ comes to reign a thousand years; there will be every sort of sect and party, and every individual following what he supposes to be the best in religion, and in everything else, similar to what it is now. Will there be wickedness then as now? No. . . . [T]he veil of the covering may be taken from before the nations, and all flesh see [Christ's] glory together, and at the same time declare they will not serve Him. . . . [During the Millennium] the different sects of Christendom [will not] be allowed to persecute each other. What will they do? They will hear of the wisdom of Zion, and . . . will come up to Zion to inquire after the ways of the Lord, and to seek out the great knowledge,

wisdom, and understanding manifested through the Saints of the Most High. They will inform the people of God that they belong to such and such a church, and do not wish to change their religion" (ibid., 2:316). President Young also taught that although "all nations . . . . will be obliged to acknowledge [Jesus'] kingly government" during the Millennium, yet "there will still be millions on the earth who will not believe in Him" (ibid., 7:142). Likewise, Joseph Fielding Smith taught that "some members of the Church have an erroneous idea that when the millennium comes all of the people are going to be swept off the earth except righteous members of the Church. That is not so. There will be millions of people, Catholics, Protestants, agnostics, [Muslims], people of all classes, and of all beliefs, still permitted to remain upon the face of the earth, but they will be those who have lived clean lives, those who have been free from wickedness and corruption. All who belong, by virtue of their good lives, to the terrestrial order, as well as those who have kept the celestial law, will remain upon the face of the earth during the millennium" (*DS,* 1:86).

40. Neal A. Maxwell, *Sermons Not Spoken* (Salt Lake City: Bookcraft, 1985), 81.

41. *CHMR,* 2:172. Similarly, James E. Talmage states: "Two gathering centers are distinctively mentioned, and the maintenance of a separate autonomy for the ancient kingdoms of Judah and Israel is repeatedly affirmed in scripture, with Jerusalem and Zion as the respective capitals. In the light of modern revelation, by which many ancient passages are illumined and made clear, we hold that the Jerusalem of Judea is to be rebuilt by the reassembled house of Judah, and that Zion is to be built up on the American continent by the gathered hosts of Israel, other than the Jews. When such shall have been accomplished, Christ shall personally rule in the earth, and then shall be realized the glad fulfillment: 'For out of Zion shall go forth the law, and the word of the Lord from Jerusalem' (Isa. 2:3; see also Joel 3:16; Zeph. 3:14)" [*VM,* 167].

42. *NWAF,* 587.

43. *WJS,* 67; emphasis added. This statement by the Prophet seems to support an idea proffered by Bruce R. McConkie, who interprets the phrase in Isaiah 2:3—"out of Zion shall go forth the law"—to mean that the New Jerusalem will be "the seat of government," and the phrase "the word of the Lord from Jerusalem" to mean that Old Jerusalem will be "the spiritual capital of the world" (Bruce R. McConkie, *The Mortal Messiah* [Salt Lake City: Deseret Book, 1979], 1:95).

44. Orson F. Whitney, *Saturday Night Thoughts* (Salt Lake City: Deseret News Press, 1921), 35.

CHAPTER 4

It Is Finished

The Millennium is destined to be a blessed age for all mankind—a time of peace, righteousness, unity, learning, and love. It will be a period of sanctification and rest, a day when the Son of the Most High will administer the kingdom of His Father with a perfect balance of mercy and justice. It will be an era when the Savior redeems all things that have been put into His power and finishes the work assigned to Him in the premortal councils of heaven (see D&C 77:12).

When the thousand years of Jesus Christ's reign are drawing to a close, a series of four major events will take place that will again change all of the temporal creations of God. These events listed in Revelation 20:5, 7–13, include the last battle with the forces of evil, the resurrection of the unjust, the Final Judgment, and the transformation of the earth into a celestial sphere. This chapter examines each of these topics as it draws from insights provided in numerous scriptural texts and also in the writings and sermons of the Lord's authorized representatives.

The Battle of the Great God

It is almost incredulous to think that after Jesus Christ removes wickedness from the world during His Second Coming, and institutes a theocratic way of governing the inhabitants of the earth, some men and women will degenerate to such a level that they will freely choose a path leading them indisputably to destruction. Yet, this is the pattern of behavior followed so frequently in the Book of Mormon, scripture that can serve as a prototype to show how events will unfold during the last days of the Millennium.[1]

The book of 4 Nephi, in the Book of Mormon, is a single chapter consisting of fewer than fifty verses. Notwithstanding its diminutive size, it contains a wealth of information preserved for the benefit and instruction of present and future generations. This text describes the conditions of the Nephites and Lamanites immediately after the resurrected Messiah appeared unto them in the Americas following His resurrection.

According to this text in 4 Nephi, the Church of Christ was established in all lands (see v. 1), and the covenant people were unified through conversion to the truth (see v. 2). There were no contentions among the Saints, and they dealt justly with one another (see v. 2, 13, 15, 18). Because these people had all things common, there were no rich or poor people, and all were free (see v. 3). Under these conditions peace was enjoyed and continued in the land (see v. 4). "There were no envyings, nor strifes, nor tumults, nor whoredoms, nor lyings, nor murders, nor any manner of lasciviousness" among this blessed group. "There were no robbers [meaning secret combinations] . . . nor [were there] any manner of –ites [or divisions of people into factions]; but they were in one, the children of Christ, and heirs to the kingdom of God" (v. 16–17).

As a group, the Saints prospered exceedingly, and they rebuilt the cities that had been destroyed immediately preceding the appearance of the Lord to them (see v. 7). They also became physically strong and multiplied exceedingly quickly (see v. 10, 16).

Scripture indicates that these individuals became so religiously devout (see v. 12) that marvelous miracles were performed in the name of Jesus Christ among them (see v. 5, 13). When they died, it is said, each one qualified for entrance into Paradise beyond the veil (see v. 14).

Then came a critical turning point that eventually led to the downfall and destruction of a people whose ancestors had literally knelt at the feet of the God of Israel. One hundred ninety-four years after the Lord Jesus Christ had taken mortality upon Himself, a small part of His ancient American followers revolted from the Church and decided to separate themselves from it by taking on an identity that historically had symbolized division (see v. 20). Then many people became exceedingly rich and prosperous (v. 23), with the prideful wearing costly apparel and other fine things (see v. 24). The Saints no longer had all things in common (see v. 25), instigating a class among them (see v. 26).

Some people began to deny the true Church, going so far as to decide which parts of the gospel they would believe. In their downward spiral, they accepted wickedness and administered the sacrament to unworthy individuals (see v. 26–27). Satan gained a firm hold on the hearts of these misguided people (see v. 28), ultimately causing them to build up churches for the sake of getting worldly gain (see v. 26).

After a time, another church arose which allowed "all manner of iniquity" (v. 34), denied Jesus Christ outright, and persecuted the true Church. Evil in its nature, this church sought to kill the Saints of God (see v. 31–33). Adherents to this clan not only hardened their hearts against the miracles they saw performed by the faithful disciples of Jesus Christ, they actually despised this power (see v. 29–30, 34). Not surprisingly, false priests and false prophets among them encouraged this hardening of heart (see v. 34).

Eventually, a great division took place among the general population (see v. 35), with those who rejected the gospel willfully rebelling against it and teaching their children to hate the true believers in Jesus Christ (see v. 38–39). Now more numerous than the people of God (see v. 40), the wicked continued to build up ornate churches unto themselves (see v. 41), but they ensured their demise when they reintroduced secret combinations (see v. 42). The outcome was devastating; there was war between the two divisions of the people (see Morm. 1:8–10).

As the Millennium progresses, this same overall pattern is expected to occur. In Doctrine and Covenants 29:22, the Lord indicates that "when the thousand years are ended . . . men [will] again begin to deny their God." When this point is reached, the Lord says He will "spare the earth but for a little season." Another scriptural reference in the Doctrine and Covenants explains why men will choose to deny their Creator, stating that "when [Satan] is loosed again he shall only reign for a little season, and then cometh the end of the earth" (D&C 43:31). John the Revelator describes what Satan will do once he is released from his bondage: "And when the thousand years are expired, Satan shall be loosed out of his prison. And shall go out to deceive the nations which are in the four quarters of the earth, Gog and Magog, to gather them together to battle: the number of whom is as the sand of the sea" (Rev. 20:7–8). Thus, the arch-deceiver "shall be loosed for a little season, that he may gather together his armies" (D&C 88:111) and prepare for the last battle.

These armies will not include just those terrestrial individuals who reside "in the four quarters of the earth," as noted, but they will also have "the hosts of hell" among their ranks (D&C 88:113). This battle is centered on the kingship of the Messiah, which the devil so desperately desires to possess (see D&C 88:115; cf. Abr. 3:27–28), and it will take place where the throne of the King resides—the "beloved city" called New Jerusalem (Rev. 20:9). Satan will direct a clan of mortal and immortal sons of perdition,[2] while the archangel Michael will lead the Lord's host (see D&C 88:112). This, in essence, will be a repeat of the war fought during premortal times, with the same commanders contending against one another (see Rev. 12:7–9). Although it will be the Saints living in and near the city of New Jerusalem who will be under attack, it will be the Almighty who defends them by sending fire from heaven to devour their terrestrial enemy (see Rev. 20:9), while Michael, or Adam, defeats the threat approaching from the other side of the veil (see D&C 88:115). The losers of this fight will endure eternal torment in a lake of fire and brimstone (see Rev. 20:10), with the result being that they will never again have power over the Saints of the living God (see D&C 88:114).

Resurrection of the Unjust

Numerous times in the Doctrine and Covenants, the Savior reveals that His grand design is to subdue all enemies under His feet when He reigns as King on the earth (see D&C 58:22; 49:6; 76:61). The Apostle Paul explains that the last enemy the Lord will put under His feet during His millennial rule is death (see 1 Cor. 15:24–26). Indeed, the Lord proclaims in the book of Revelation that He holds possession of the key of death (see Rev. 1:18).

As noted in the previous chapter, the resurrection of the just (those who merit the celestial and terrestrial kingdoms) is to be accomplished at and near the beginning of the Millennium. The resurrection of the unjust, however, will not take place until the end of Christ's reign, after the thousand years have ended (see Rev. 20:5; D&C 88:101). Nevertheless, the inheritors of telestial bodies and the sons of perdition will come forth from their graves "before the earth shall pass away" (D&C 29:26). In fact, Joseph Fielding Smith specifies, "The resurrection of the wicked will take place as one of the last events before the earth dies."[3]

Identification of the Unjust

When the New Testament speaks of the "resurrection . . . of the . . . unjust" in Acts 24:15, the Greek word translated as "unjust" is *adikos,* and it is used in referring to a "wicked" person. This word is also translated in the King James Bible as "unrighteous."[4] In Doctrine and Covenants 76 those individuals who come up in the resurrection of the unjust are labeled as "evil" (D&C 76:17). Another modern revelation relates that they will be placed at

Christ's left hand—a place of dishonor—and they will be commanded to depart from His presence because He will be ashamed to own them before God the Father (see D&C 29:27–28).

Those persons who earn a resurrection with a telestial body will be they who are found to be under condemnation (see D&C 88:100–101) because they reject the prophets, the gospel, the everlasting covenant, and the testimony of Jesus. They are those who love lies and make them, engage in unlawful sexual conduct, and advocate false power. They will have to suffer the wrath of Almighty God in hell until Christ will have subdued all enemies and perfected His work. Their glory will be dim—like the light that emanates from the stars. And they will be banished forever from the presence of the Father and the Son (see D&C 76:99–106, 109–112).

The Most Unjust of All

Mortals who become sons of perdition are the most unjust of all God's creations because they have allowed themselves to be overcome by the power of the devil after partaking of the power of God. Sons of perdition act as traitors to all that is good by denying the truth and openly defying God's power. They cannot gain forgiveness and are thus doomed to suffer the wrath of God for all eternity. In their situation, they would have been better off had they never been born (see D&C 76:28–38). When these wretched individuals come forth from the grave, they will be "filthy still" because there is no way for them to be cleansed by the Atonement of the Savior (see D&C 88:102).

The Great Day of Judgment

The scriptures prophesy that the time will come when all men and women will be judged for how they lived during mortality. Elder

John A. Widtsoe writes: "The time must come in the eternal hereafter, the day of judgment, when every human being will be judged by the way he carried out on earth his pre-existent agreement with the Lord." We all "came down on earth with the possibility of winning access to the greatest blessings of God," says Elder Widtsoe. And we will be evaluated by how far we have approached that goal or, in other words, how we stand after earth-life in comparison to our premortal condition. "As effect follows cause, so the answers to such questions will determine the gains of the man [or woman] from [their] earth-experience."[5]

Jacob, the brother of the prophet Nephi, refers to the chronology of the Final Judgment in the book of 2 Nephi. He says that "it shall come to pass that when all men shall have passed from this first death unto life [i.e., in the resurrection], insomuch as they have become immortal, they must appear before the judgment-seat of the Holy One of Israel; and then cometh the judgment, and then must they be judged according to the holy judgment of God" (2 Ne. 9:15). Thus, the time of ultimate reckoning and recognition before Deity will occur sometime after mankind has risen from the grave.

Appearance of a Herald Angel

The Lord states in section 88 of the Doctrine and Covenants that before the Final Judgment begins, a heavenly herald will announce it and then every man and woman will make a physical acknowledgment of the approaching event. An angel will sound a trumpet that will be heard in heaven, on earth, and under the earth (meaning that every ear will hear it), and then "every knee shall bow, and every tongue shall confess, while they hear the sound of the trump, saying: 'Fear God, and give glory to Him who sitteth upon the throne, forever and ever; for the hour of His judgment is come'" (v. 104). It will be the Son of God, acting in His capacity as King, who will be seated upon the throne of judgment, for God the Father has "given Him authority to execute judgment"; the

Father has "committed all judgment unto the Son" (John 5:22, 27). Indeed, the Savior Himself has taught that when the Son of Man comes in His glory He will "sit upon the throne of His glory" and then proceed to separate the sheep from the goats and assign them their reward (Matt. 25:31–46).

Judgment and Reward

Some of the criteria for judgment can be found in the prophecies of the Apostle John. He relates one of the things that he glimpsed in his vision of the future: "And I saw the dead, small and great, stand before God; and the books were opened: and another book was opened, which is the book of life: and the dead were judged out of those things which were written in the books, according to their works" (Rev. 20:12). But these are not the only criteria on which the Final Judgment will be based. James E. Talmage affirms that "every man will be called to answer for his deeds; and not for deeds alone but for his words also and even for the thoughts of his heart."[6]

Four general categories of reward will be handed out on the day of judgment. Each individual will inherit the celestial, terrestrial, or telestial kingdom or will be consigned to reside forever in outer darkness. It appears that Jesus Christ referred to each of these four places when He spoke the following prophetic words to John the Revelator: "He that is unjust, let him be unjust till [i.e., the telestial kingdom]: and he which is filthy, let him be filthy still [i.e., outer darkness]: and he that is righteous, let him be righteous still [i.e., the terrestrial kingdom]: and he that is holy, let him be holy still [i.e., the celestial kingdom]. And, behold, I come quickly; and my reward is with me, to give every man according as his work shall be" (Rev. 22:11–12; cf. Morm. 9:13–14).

Once the Final Judgment has been completed, the inhabitants of the earth may expect to see the fulfillment of a prophecy found in Doctrine and Covenants 88:108–110. According to this scripture, the time will come when a series of seven angels will sound trumpets "in the ears of all living, and reveal the secret acts of men [including their thoughts and the intents of their hearts], and [also] the mighty works of God" that have taken place during a period of seven thousand years. Each of the trumpet blasts is to precede the revelation of human acts and heavenly works during a thousand-year timeframe. It seems logical that this event will take place after the secret acts of men have been laid bare at the judgment bar of the Lord Jesus Christ.

The Earth Becomes Celestial

After the dead have all been removed from the bowels and elements of the earth—through the process of resurrection—then it will be time for the planet to undergo a change greater than that which occurred when it was crowned with the presence of the glorified Son of Man.

The earth, as taught in modern revelation, fills the measure of its creation and does not transgress; therefore, it abides the law of a celestial kingdom. In consequence of these conditions, the earth is worthy of receiving "celestial glory" and becoming the eternal abode of those resurrected "bodies who are of the celestial kingdom." This is the intent for which the earth was created. The process of the transition from a terrestrial world to a celestial kingdom is outlined briefly in the scriptures. The Doctrine and Covenants reveals that the earth will actually "die" and be "quickened again" by the celestial power (D&C 88:18–20, 25–26). Another passage of scripture states that "when the thousand years are ended . . . the end shall come, and the heaven and the earth shall be consumed and pass away, and there shall be a new heaven and a new earth" (D&C 29:23–24). This consumption was described by Jesus Christ during His mortal ministry to the Nephites. He taught them that "the elements [will] melt with fervent heat, and the earth [will] be wrapt together as a scroll, and the heavens and the earth [will] pass away" (3 Ne. 26:3; cf. Morm. 9:2). John the Revelator was given the opportunity to see a representation of the earth's death. In his panoramic vision of the future, he "saw a great white throne, and Him that sat on it, from whose face the earth and the heaven fled away; and there was found no place for them" (Rev. 20:11). Thus, the earth will be changed to a higher plane of existence through the agency of divine power. Orson Pratt proposes the following thoughts concerning this cataclysmic, but necessary, transformation:

> The earth itself is to pass through a similar change to that which we have to pass through. As our bodies return again to mother dust, forming constituent portions thereof, and no place is found for them as organized bodies, so it will be with this earth. Not only will the elements melt with fervent heat, but the great globe itself will pass away. It will cease to exist as an organized world. It will cease to exist as one of the worlds that are capable of being inhabited. Fire devours all things, converting the earth into its original elements; it passes away into space.
>
> But not one particle of the elements which compose the earth will be destroyed or annihilated. They will all exist and be brought together again by a greater organizing power than is known to man. The earth must be resurrected again, as well as our bodies; its elements will be reunited, and they will be brought together by the power of God's word.[7]

Brigham Young declares that "when [the earth] becomes celestialized, it will be like the sun, and be prepared for the habitation of the Saints, and be brought back into the presence of the Father and the Son. It will not then be an opaque body as it now is, but it will be . . . full of light and glory; it will be a body of light."[8] "This earth, in its sanctified and immortal state," explains the Prophet Joseph Smith, "will be made like unto crystal and will be a Urim and Thummim to the inhabitants who dwell thereon, whereby all things pertaining to an inferior kingdom, or all kingdoms of a lower order, will be manifest to those who dwell on it" (D&C 130:9). Aside from this quality of infused revelatory capacity, the earth will maintain some similarity with its present state. Again Orson Pratt offers insight:

> A Saint who is one in deed and truth, does not look for an immaterial heaven, but he expects a heaven with lands, houses, cities, vegetation, rivers, and animals; with thrones, temples, palaces, kings, princes, priests, and angels; with food, raiment, musical instruments, etc., all of which are material. Indeed, the Saints' heaven is a redeemed, glorified, celestial, material creation inhabited by glorified material beings, male and female, organized into families, embracing all the relationships of husbands and wives, parents and children, where sorrow, crying, pain, and death will be known no more. Or to speak still more definitely, this earth, when glorified, is the Saints' eternal heaven. On it they expect to live, with body, parts, and holy passions; on it they expect to move and have their being; to eat, drink, converse, worship, sing, play on musical instruments, engage in joyful, innocent, social amusements, visit neighboring towns and neighboring worlds; indeed, matter and its qualities and properties are the only beings or things with which they expect to associate.[9]

A preview of the earth in its celestial mode is provided in the prophecies of the Apostle John. He saw by vision—as recorded in the 20th and 21st chapters of the book of Revelation[10]—that it will be a place where there is no curse, as there has been upon the earth since the fall of Adam and Eve (see Rev. 22:3). In consequence of this, there will be no death, no sorrow, no crying, and no pain will be found anywhere on earth (see Rev. 21:4). The earth will exist as a place of holiness, for nothing on it will defile or work abomination or lies (see Rev. 21:27).

Such a place is a fit habitation for Deity. In fact, the Apostle John wrote that God Himself will dwell upon the celestialized earth (see Rev. 21:3), and the inhabitants of it will "see His face" (Rev. 22:4). The throne of the Almighty will be there (see Rev. 22:3) and His glory will radiate throughout its environs (see Rev. 21:23).

John notes that individuals who inherit this supremely holy place will be those whose names are written in the Lamb's book of life (see Rev. 21:27)—people who kept the commandments of the Lord (see Rev. 22:14). The men will hold the office of "kings" (see Rev. 21:24) and be granted the title of "son" in the family of the Father (Rev. 21:7). Indeed, the Revelator reports that even the name of God Himself will be found emblazoned upon their foreheads (see Rev. 22:4), as they have overcome their trials and thus qualify to inherit all things (see Rev. 21:7).

Two aspects of John's apocalyptic description offer more knowledge about the celestial earth. The city of New Jerusalem has a prominent place in his word-picture, and in the Doctrine and Covenants it is reported that those individuals who "die in the Lord" will eventually "receive an inheritance before the Lord, *in the holy city*" (D&C 63:49; emphasis added). It is "the poor and the meek of the earth," affirms modern holy writ, who "shall inherit it" (D&C 88:17). Continued perusal of latter-day scripture reveals that the reception of inheritances will take place after an angel of God sounds his trumpet and proclaims, "It is finished; it is finished! The Lamb of God hath overcome and trodden the winepress alone" (D&C 88:106–107). At this point, the work of the Savior will be perfected; He will deliver up the kingdom to His

Father and will echo the words pronounced by the heralding angel—"I have overcome and have trodden the winepress alone." The Messiah will then be crowned and enthroned to reign for eternity; the angels will be crowned with the glory of His might; and the Saints will be filled with His glory insomuch that they are made "equal with Him" (D&C 88:106–107; 76:106–108).

The most significant point mentioned by John the Revelator is that once the earth is infused with "celestial glory," it is to be "crowned . . . with the presence of God the Father" (D&C 88:18–19). The Almighty "will dwell with man upon the [celestial] earth." Orson Pratt asks, "Will this confine Him to this earth?" and answers, "No, not any more than the kings of the earth are confined to their palaces, or the city in which they may dwell." When we think of earthly monarchs, we understand that "they have the right to visit the different portions of their dominions and even any parts of the earth. So will God our Eternal Father, when He selects this earth as a habitation, make it as one of His dwelling places, but He will have power to go from one celestial world to another, to visit the myriads of [His] creations, as may seem to Him good."[11] And if it so happens that God is physically absent from any particular celestial sphere, Elder Pratt postulates, then the sanctified and exalted inhabitants of that orb would be in His presence nevertheless—with the ability to both see and converse with Him. It is only the veil that prevents any person from viewing things at a great distance with their spiritual eyes. Without the veil intervening as an obstacle, explains Elder Pratt, "all the [celestial] creations that are redeemed can enjoy the continued and eternal presence of the Lord their God," though He be millions of miles distant from their physical location.[12]

Notes to Chapter 4

1. "Perhaps the best model to help [us to] understand how this can happen is the demise of the near millennial society found in 4 Nephi and Mormon 1 in the Book of Mormon" (*OSS,* 221). "[T]he destruction of the world (meaning the wicked) and the glory of Christ's second coming are set forth figuratively in the events of Third Nephi, just as the millennium is prefigured in the first part of Fourth Nephi" (Richard D. Rust, *Feasting on the Word: The Literary Testimony of the Book of Mormon* [Salt Lake City: Deseret Book, 1997], 7).

2. *DS,* 1:87; *JD*, 16:322.

3. *DS,* 1:87.

4. *SSECB,* 1476, Greek Dictionary, word #94.

5. John A. Widtsoe, *Joseph Smith—Seeker after Truth, Prophet of God* (Salt Lake City: Deseret News Press, 1951), 171.

6. *SAE,* 55.

7. *JD,* 18:346–47.

8. Ibid., 7:163.

9. *Masterful Discourses and Writings of Orson Pratt* (Salt Lake City: Bookcraft, 1962), 62–63.

10. Some General Authorities who see Revelation chapters 20 and 21 as a description of the celestialized earth include Joseph Fielding Smith, *AGQ,* 2:103–6; Harold B. Lee in Clyde J. Williams, ed., *The Teachings of Harold B. Lee* (Salt Lake City: Bookcraft, 1996), 78; John Taylor, *The Government of God* (Liverpool, England: S. W. Richards, 1852), 42; Orson Pratt, *JD,* 16:322–23; Bruce R. McConkie, *The Millennial Messiah,* 693–705.

11. *JD,* 18:322.

12. Ibid., 17:332–33.

CHAPTER 5

OIL IN OUR LAMPS

One of the prominent and recurring themes imbedded in scriptures that mention the signs of the times, the Second Coming, and the Millennium is that of preparation. Throughout the pages of canonized writings a resounding cry is made: "Prepare ye, prepare ye, O inhabitants of the earth; for the judgment of our God is come" (D&C 88:92); "prepare for the revelation which is to come, when . . . all flesh shall see [the Savior] together" (D&C 101:22–23); "prepare yourselves for the great day of the Lord" (D&C 133:10).

On one occasion when Bruce R. McConkie spoke to the worldwide audience of Latter-day Saints in general conference, he emphasized this important theme, reminding the Saints that preparation must be on more than just one level:

> I stand before the Church this day and raise the warning voice. It is a prophetic voice, for I shall say only what the apostles and prophets have spoken concerning our day. . . .
>
> It is a voice calling upon the Lord's people to prepare for the troubles and desolations which are about to be poured out upon the world without measure.
>
> For the moment we live in a day of peace and prosperity but it shall not ever be thus. Great trials

> lie ahead. All of the sorrows and perils of the past are but a foretaste of what is yet to be. And we must prepare ourselves temporally and spiritually. . . .
>
> Peace has been taken from the earth, the angels of destruction have begun their work, and their swords shall not be sheathed until the Prince of Peace comes to destroy the wicked and usher in the great millennium.[1]

Three successive parables of preparation in the book of Matthew all reflect the chronology of events awaiting each of the Lord's children in the last days. The first is the parable of the ten virgins (see Matt. 25:1–13), representing preparation for Christ's arrival. Immediately following it is the parable of the talents (see Matt. 25:14–30), representing preparation for rendering an account of one's stewardship. And the final parable is that of the sheep and the goats (see Matt. 25:31–46), representing preparation for the Final Judgment.[2]

It is probably not by coincidence that these parables were spoken by the Savior in the order in which they appear in the New Testament. Indeed, they foreshadow events that all men and women will experience during the last days and beyond.

The Parable of the Ten Virgins

Through modern revelation the Lord has indicated that the parable of the ten virgins is actually a prophecy, and He has stated that when He comes to the earth in His glory this prophecy will be fulfilled. He then makes an explicit identification of the five wise virgins by saying that they are the ones who have "received the truth," "taken the Holy Spirit for their guide," and "have not been deceived." These individuals will "abide the day" of the Second Coming or, to speak in symbolic terms, "they shall not be hewn down and cast into the fire" (D&C 45:56–57). Nevertheless, as the Lord explains, "Until [the] hour [of the coming of the Son of Man] there will be foolish virgins among the wise" (D&C 63:54).

President Wilford Woodruff pointedly remarks about this parable and the disciples of Jesus Christ who belong to His restored Church:

> The parable of the ten virgins is intended to represent the second coming of the Son of Man, the coming of the Bridegroom to meet the bride, the Church, the Lamb's wife, in the last days; and I expect that the Savior was about right when He said, in reference to the members of the Church, that five of them were wise and five were foolish; for when the Lord of heaven comes in power and great glory to reward every man according to the deeds done in the body, if He finds one half of those professing to be members of His Church prepared for salvation, it will be as many as can be expected, judging by the course that many are pursuing.[3]

The obligation laid upon the Latter-day Saints is to let their voices be heard "among all people" (including the foolish virgins), saying, "Awake and arise and go forth to meet the Bridegroom; behold and lo, the Bridegroom cometh; go ye out to meet Him. Prepare yourselves for the great day of the Lord" (D&C 133:10, 19; cf. 65:3). The angels of God will voice the same proclamation immediately before the sign of the Son of Man appears. The Lord's messengers will fly through the midst of heaven and cry with a loud voice, "Prepare ye, prepare ye, O inhabitants of the earth; for the judgment of our God is come. Behold, and lo, the Bridegroom cometh; go ye out to meet Him" (D&C 88:92).

The advice of the Lord to those who desire to be counted among the wise virgins is simple: "Wherefore, be faithful, praying always, having your lamps trimmed and burning, and oil with you, that you may be ready at the coming of the Bridegroom" (D&C 33:17). Those who qualify to be counted among the wise virgins have specific promises made to them by the Lord. In the Doctrine and Covenants, He says that "the earth shall be given unto them for an inheritance; and they shall multiply and wax strong, and their children shall grow up without sin unto salvation. For the Lord shall be in their midst, and His glory shall be upon them, and He will be their king and their lawgiver" (D&C 45:58–59). Since General Authorities such as Spencer W. Kimball, Wilford Woodruff, and Dallin H. Oaks[4] identify the virgins in this parable as members of the LDS Church, it follows that these precious promises apply to them and that their desire should be to share them with others by calling on them to "awake and arise."

But how do individuals supply oil for their lamps so that they may be counted among the wise in the day when the Lord of Hosts descends to the earth? Again, President Wilford Woodruff offers counsel.

> [W]e keep oil in our lamps . . . by keeping the commandments of God, remembering our prayers, doing as we are told by the revelations of Jesus Christ, and otherwise assisting in building up Zion. When we are laboring for the kingdom of God, we will have oil in our lamps, our light will shine and we will feel the testimony of the Spirit of God. On the other hand, if we set our hearts upon the things of the world and seek for the honors of men, we shall walk in the dark and not in the light. If we do not value our priesthood, and the work of this priesthood, the building up of the kingdom of God, the rearing of temples, the redeeming of our dead, and the carrying out of the great work unto which we have been ordained by the God of Israel—if we do not feel that these things are more valuable to us

> than the things of the world, we will have no oil in our lamps, no light, and we shall fail to be present at the marriage supper of the Lamb.[5]

The Parable of the Talents

In the parable of the talents, which is representative of the kingdom of heaven, the "wicked and slothful" servant fails to make adequate preparation for his master's return. After he reports his negligent stewardship, he is cast out to a place of weeping and darkness. The other two servants, on the other hand, are found to be "good and faithful" in relation to their stewardships. They prepare prudently for their master's return even though it takes "a long time" for that return to come about. Consequently, they were rewarded with positions of rulership over greater things than that with which they initially had been entrusted. The "faithful and wise servant" and the "evil servant" motifs are also spotlighted in chapter 24 of the Joseph Smith Translation of Matthew, which focuses specifically on the last days. Here the Savior repeats the idea that the evil servant is the one who thinks that the lord "delayeth His coming" and finds out to his detriment that the lord comes "in a day when [the evil servant] looketh not for Him, and in an hour [that] he is not aware of." The "wise servant," conversely, will be "blessed" when his lord finds him doing his assigned tasks or fulfilling his stewardship. The reward for the faithful is very great, even that of becoming a "ruler" over many things (v. 51–56).

In modern revelation, the Lord provides additional insight about these teachings, giving more-than-adequate incentive for our personal preparation when He announces that "it is required of the Lord, at the hand of every steward, to render an account of his stewardship, both in time and in eternity. For he who is faithful and wise in time is accounted worthy to inherit the mansions prepared for him of my Father" (D&C 72:3–4). And in other sections of the Doctrine and Covenants, He reiterates the fact that

He will eventually require stewardships at the hands of each individual (see D&C 104:11–12; 124:14).

In June 1965, President David O. McKay explained what will be required of individuals when they are called forward to account for that over which they were made stewards. Because of the nature of President McKay's instructions, they may rightly be considered as a type of prophecy. To the male members of the Church, he said:

> Let me assure you, brethren, that someday you will have a personal priesthood interview with the Savior Himself. If you are interested, I will tell you the order in which He will ask you to account for your earthly responsibilities.
>
> First, He will request an accountability report about your relationship with your wife. Have you actively been engaged in making her happy and ensuring that her needs have been met as an individual?
>
> Second, He will want an accountability report about each of your children individually. He will not attempt to have this for simply a family stewardship but will request information about your relationship to each and every child.
>
> Third, He will want to know what you personally have done with the talents you were given in the preexistence.
>
> Fourth, He will want a summary of your activity in your Church assignments. He will not be necessarily interested in what assignments you have had, for in His eyes the home teacher and a mission president are probably equals, but He will request a summary of how you have been of service to your fellowmen in your Church assignments.

> Fifth, He will have no interest in how you earned your living, but [instead in whether] you were honest in all your dealings.
>
> Sixth, He will ask for an accountability on what you have done to contribute in a positive manner to your community, state, country and the world.[6]

The Parable of the Sheep and the Goats

The last parable in this series is that of the sheep and the goats. In this parable, Jesus Christ is likened unto a shepherd who, when He comes the second time, will separate the sheep from the goats among all nations while He is enthroned (a clear reference to judgment being rendered by a king). The sheep take their place at the right hand of the shepherd; they are "blessed" and inherit the kingdom of the Father. The goats take their place on the left hand of the shepherd; they are "cursed" and cast out with the devil and his followers. The Lord specifies that those who are found on His left hand will suffer "weeping, wailing and gnashing of teeth"; they will be subjected to "woes" because they choose not to repent (D&C 19:4–5).

The question might be asked, How should Latter-day Saints prepare themselves to be counted among the sheep instead of the goats during the Final Judgment? The way is pointed out in simplicity within the text of the parable itself. According to the Son of God, true Saints who are prepared will (1) give food to the hungry and water to the thirsty, (2) provide shelter and clothing for the needy, and (3) minister unto the sick and imprisoned.

The Lord considers such charitable service for the benefit of His brethren as if it were being done for Him. As aptly stated in the Book of Mormon, those who are in the service of their fellow beings are considered to be in the service of God (see Mosiah 2:17). And the reward for engaging in freewill service is to be "blessed" by the Creator of heaven and earth with a blessing with eternal ramifications. Those who fail to act in mortality with a benevolent heart will also receive the recompense for which they qualify. As a reminder, Spencer W. Kimball states that "no one will escape the reward of his deeds. No one will fail to receive the blessings earned. . . . [T]he parable of the sheep and goats gives us assurance that there will be total justice."[7] To be counted among the sheep when the Lord comes and plumbs the depths of mortal souls will require a sincere effort to bless the lives of others. "I do pray that the Lord will bless those who are lukewarm, who are indifferent, and uninterested in the work of the Lord," said President Joseph F. Smith, "that they may awaken to their duty and learn to earn the reward of the faithful, that they may not be ignored when God shall choose His own and set the sheep on His right hand, and the goats on the left, and shall say to the latter 'depart from me.'"[8]

Looking to the Future

Responding to the wish of some individuals to be born in some dispensation other than that of the latter days, President Harold B. Lee expressed his enthusiasm to live during an eventful period of world history. "Remember," said President Lee, "that all this is as the putting forth of the buds of the trees, reminding us that summer is not far distant" (see Luke 21:29–31). "For the Latter-day Saints," President Lee emphasized, "this is the day of preparation to put oil in our lamps and prepare ourselves for the coming of the Bridegroom. In that day when the wicked shall be swept from the earth, we who are prepared shall enjoy that great millennium of peace."[9]

Undeniably, there are numerous frightening experiences ahead for humanity in the last days. Yet the leaders of the Lord's restored Church offer a message of encouragement and hope for the future. President Howard W. Hunter, an example of one such leader, readily admits that "the scriptures . . . indicate that there will be seasons of time when the whole world will have some difficulty."

He also acknowledges that "in our dispensation unrighteousness will, unfortunately, be quite evident, and it will bring its inevitable difficulties and pain and punishment." Yet he teaches that

> our task is to live fully and faithfully and not worry ourselves sick about the woes of the world or when it will end. Our task is to have the gospel in our lives and to be a bright light, a city set upon a hill that reflects the beauty of the gospel of Jesus Christ and the joy and happiness that will always come to every people in every age who keep the commandments.
>
> In this last dispensation there will be great tribulation (Matt. 24:21). We know that from the scriptures. We know there will be wars and rumors of wars and that the whole earth will be in commotion (D&C 45:26). All dispensations have had their perilous times, but our day will include genuine peril (2 Tim. 3:1). Evil men will flourish (2 Tim. 3:13), but then evil men have very often flourished. Calamities will come and iniquity will abound (D&C 45:27).
>
> Inevitably, the natural result of some of these kinds of prophecies is fear, and that is not fear limited to a younger generation. It is fear shared by those of any age who don't understand what we understand.
>
> But I want to stress that these feelings are not necessary for faithful Latter-day Saints, and they do not come from God.[10]

Jeffrey R. Holland focuses on this same issue. In speaking about the dangers and alarming conditions of the last days, he counsels that

> We must *never,* in *any* age or circumstance, let fear and the father of fear (Satan himself) divert us from our faith and faithful living. There have *always* been questions about the future. Every young person or every young couple in every era has had to walk by faith into what has *always* been some uncertainty—starting with Adam and Eve in those first tremulous steps out of the Garden of Eden. But that is all right. This is the plan. It will be okay. Just be faithful. God is in charge. He knows your name and He knows your need.[11]

Similar thoughts are expressed by M. Russell Ballard, who says,

> The prophecies of the last days lead me to believe that the intensity of the battle for the souls of men will increase and the risks will become greater as we draw closer to the second coming of the Lord. . . . Preparing ourselves and our families for the challenges of the coming years will require us to replace fear with faith. We must be able to overcome the fear of enemies who oppose and threaten us. The Lord has said, "Fear not, little flock; do good; let earth and hell combine against you, for if ye are built upon my rock, they cannot prevail" (D&C 6:34).[12]

There are two general types of preparation that Latter-day Saints can engage in so that when they are called upon to pass through the trials of the last days, they can more easily deal with those ordeals. All members of the Church can prepare inwardly and outwardly.

Inward preparation includes the mental equipping of the heart and mind; it is centered on how one thinks and how one feels.

President Ezra Taft Benson underscores the fact that "too often we bask in our comfortable complacency and rationalize that the ravages of war, economic disaster, famine, and earthquake cannot happen" where we live. This, in the view of President Benson, is a mistake. "Those who believe this," he says, "are either not acquainted with the revelations of the Lord, or they do not believe them." As a result, "those who smugly think these calamities will not happen, that they somehow will be set aside because of the righteousness of the Saints, are deceived and will rue the day they harbored such a delusion."[13] President George Albert Smith states that in addition to a realistic state of mind, one must also put his spiritual life in proper order. "Though the world may be filled with distress, and the heavens gather blackness, and the vivid lightnings flash, and the earth quake from center to circumference," he declares, "if we know that God lives, and our lives are righteous, we will be happy; there will be peace unspeakable because we know our Father approves our lives."[14] Even though we might accept the fact that latter-day tragedies may take place in our immediate vicinity—but we feel good because our standing before the Almighty is in proper order—we still might perish if we fail to prepare outwardly. The unexpected vicissitudes of life such as injury, unemployment, disease, and natural disaster can befall anyone at anytime. In light of this verity, as noted in the *Encyclopedia of Mormonism,* adherents of the faith are encouraged to become self-sufficient and acquire the resources and skills necessary to survive and overcome these difficult challenges.

> For more than a hundred years, Church leaders have taught the members to store grain and other essentials that would sustain life in times of drought or famine (Essentials of Home Production and Storage, p. 17). The current guidelines for home storage are intended to apply internationally. They include having a supply of food, clothing, and,

> where possible, the fuel necessary to sustain life for one year.[15]

It should be remembered that it is best for families and individuals to secure themselves against possible long-term catastrophic emergencies, since the Church organization does not maintain crisis-related supplies for its entire membership. In making their preparations for unforeseen predicaments, Latter-day Saints are admonished to obtain relevant insurance where possible, avoid debt, seek educational opportunities with regard to emergency procedures, maintain good bodily health, save extra money, and avoid purchasing necessities under a sense of panic.[16] This advice parallels that given by President Gordon B. Hinckley as he once discussed the outbreak of war. In connection with the "grim warnings" found in chapter 24 of the book of Matthew, President Hinckley told the Saints that they should get free of debt, have a little money laid aside against a rainy day, and have some food set aside to sustain them in case of need. He urged the Saints, however, to "not panic nor go to extremes" in these matters but to "be prudent in every respect."[17] An epistle by the First Presidency of an earlier era draws attention back to the title and theme of this chapter; their words provide a visual imagery that can stand as a constant reminder of the need to be prepared for all that is yet to come. They admonish the members of the Church to "prepare as a bride to receive her bridegroom; let the Saints have on their wedding garments, and have their lamps well supplied with oil, trimmed and burning." In summary, "let all things be made ready for the reception of our Savior and Redeemer, even our Lord the Christ."[18]

Notes to Chapter 5

1. *Ensign,* May 1979, 92–93.
2. For an overview of this pattern, see J. Lewis Taylor, "How shall I read the parables of preparation in Matthew 25 in the context of the last days?" *Ensign,* June 1975, 22–23.
3. G. Homer Durham, ed., *The Discourses of Wilford Woodruff* (Salt Lake City: Bookcraft, 1969), 254; hereafter cited as *DWW.*
4. See Spencer W. Kimball, *Faith Precedes the Miracle* (Salt Lake City: Deseret Book, 1972), 253–54; *JD,* 18:110; *Ensign,* May 2004, 8.
5. *DWW,* 124–25.
6. Notes taken in June 1965 by Fred A. Baker, Managing Director, Department of Physical Facilities, published in Randy L. Bott, *Home with Honor* (Salt Lake City: Deseret Book, 1995), 168–69.
7. CR, Apr. 1952, 22.
8. Ibid., Apr. 1911, 10.
9. Clyde J. Williams, ed., *The Teachings of Harold B. Lee* (Salt Lake City: Bookcraft, 1996), 406.
10. Clyde J. Williams, ed., *The Teachings of Howard W. Hunter* (Salt Lake City: Bookcraft, 1997), 200–201.
11. Jeffrey R. Holland, "Terror, Triumph, and a Wedding Feast," *Brigham Young University 2004–2005 Speeches* (Provo, UT: Brigham Young University, 2005), 3; emphasis in original.
12. CR, Oct. 1989, 43.
13. *Ensign,* Nov. 1980, 34.
14. Robert McIntosh and Susan McIntosh, ed., *The Teachings of George Albert Smith* (Salt Lake City: Bookcraft, 1996), 189.
15. *Ensign,* Nov. 1995, 35–36.
16. Ibid.
17. Ibid., Nov. 2001, 73.
18. *MFP,* 2:211.

CHAPTER 6

QUESTIONS AND ANSWERS

Fortunately, Latter-day Saints have access to an abundance of resources where they can find answers to questions pertaining to the signs of the times, the Second Coming, and the Millennium. This chapter will pose and then answer some relevant questions regularly raised by members of the Church but not covered in previous portions of this book.

QUESTION 1

The Lord said back in the 1830s that the day of His coming was "nigh at hand" (D&C 35:15; 43:17; 106:4; 133:17). Isn't there a discrepancy between this declaration and the fact that the Second Coming has not yet occurred?

Answer:

Not necessarily. A similar set of circumstances is found in the Book of Mormon. In Mosiah 3:5, King Benjamin says in relation to the first coming of the Savior: "For behold, *the time cometh, and is not far distant,* that with power, the Lord Omnipotent who reigneth, who was, and is from all eternity to all eternity, *shall come down from heaven* among the children of men, and shall dwell in a tabernacle of clay, and shall go forth amongst men" (emphasis added).

Approximately 120 years elapsed between the time King Benjamin made this statement and the actual arrival of Jesus Christ on the earth. It is, therefore, reasonable to think in these same terms when considering statements found in modern scripture. However, one must also remember that the Lord Himself is speaking in the Doctrine and Covenants passages cited above. His reckoning of time is very different from man's reckoning. A single hour for the Lord is equivalent to 41.67 earth years (see the chart in chapter 2 of this book). If the Lord says that His coming is "nigh," and from His perspective it is only five hours away, then for mortals the wait would be calculated as 208.35 years.

The first chapter and first verse of the book of Revelation also provides a cautionary note relating to this issue. The Apostle John said that the events portrayed within that volume are "things which must shortly come to pass"—and yet more than two thousand years later, some of these prophecies still await fulfillment.

QUESTION 2

Do all the inhabitants of the earth need to hear the restored gospel preached unto them before the Second Coming takes place?

Answer:

Two New Testament scriptures modified by the Prophet Joseph Smith teach that the "gospel of the kingdom shall be preached in all the world, for a witness unto all nations, and then shall the end come, or the destruction of the wicked" (JST, Matt. 24:32; JST, Mark 13:36). However, this proclamation does not specify that every individual on the earth must hear the gospel personally before the Second Coming takes place, only that it will be preached "in all the world." John the Revelator provides one way to interpret this passage. In his vision of the last days, John learned that "kings and priests" would be ordained "out of every kindred, and tongue, and people, and nation" who would "reign on the earth" during the Millennium (Rev. 5:9–10). Bruce R. McConkie elaborates on this idea as follows:

> The way we become kings and priests is through the ordinances of the house of the Lord. It is

> through celestial marriage; it is through the guarantees of eternal life and eternal increase that are reserved for the Saints in the temples. When the Lord comes He is going to find in every nation and kindred, among every people speaking every tongue, those who will, at [the] hour of His coming, have already become kings and priests.[1]

Confirming the truths shown to John the Revelator relating to events of the last days, the prophet Nephi received a similar vision. He learned that the wicked influence or dominion of the great and abominable church will be so pervasive throughout the world that the Saints will be "few" in number—despite the fact that they will be scattered "upon all the face of the earth" (1 Ne. 14:9–14).

QUESTION 3

How should one understand the prophecy about the "one mighty and strong" in Doctrine and Covenants 85:7?

Answer:

On November 27, 1832, the Prophet Joseph Smith, who was at that time in Kirtland, Ohio, wrote a letter to William W. Phelps, who was residing in Independence, Missouri. In his letter, the Prophet mentioned that the Bishop of Zion—Edward Partridge—was "the man that God has appointed in a legal way, agreeably to the law given to organize and regulate the Church, and all the affairs of the same." Yet people who were moving to Zion and establishing themselves there were not receiving their inheritances by deed through the law of consecration (see D&C 51:1–4; 57:7). This situation weighed heavily upon the mind of the Prophet.

On an earlier occasion, the Lord had informed Bishop Partridge that he needed to repent or he would fall (see D&C 58:14–19). When the Prophet wrote his letter to Brother Phelps in

Zion, he repeated that message, and informed Brother Phelps that he had received a revelation from the Lord with regard to the deeding of inheritances. The Lord indicated that He would "send one mighty and strong, holding the scepter of power in his hand, clothed with light for a covering, whose mouth shall utter words, eternal words; while his bowels shall be a fountain of truth, to set in order the house of God, and to arrange by lot the inheritances of the Saints." The Lord also said that "that man, who was called of God, and appointed, that putteth forth his hand to steady the ark of God, shall fall." In other words, because the bishop of Zion was not performing his assigned task, the Lord was considering removing him and sending someone else to do the job. The Prophet remarked to Brother Phelps in his letter that "men ought to be [careful] what they do in the last days, lest they are cut short of their expectations, and they that think they stand should fall, because they keep not the Lord's commandments."[2]

From Doctrine and Covenants 90, it is evident that Edward Partridge was in the process of repentance a little over three months later (March 8, 1833), as the Lord was then directing the Prophet to send people to Bishop Partridge to establish their inheritances. Still, the Lord indicated that Bishop Partridge needed to make more progress (see v. 30, 34–35). The Saints were eventually driven from the state of Missouri by their enemies, and the issue of assigning inheritances in Zion was set aside. Apparently, by 1835, Bishop Partridge improved significantly, since the Lord announced that his sins had been forgiven.[3] And when Edward Partridge died several years later, the Lord reported that he had been accepted into the divine presence (see D&C 124:19).

In 1867, William W. Phelps informed President Brigham Young that the personage referred to in the letter he had received from the Prophet—part of which became Doctrine and Covenants 85—was Father Adam, the patriarch of the whole human family.[4] It is not known how Brother Phelps learned the identity of the "one mighty and strong," but it is clear that Adam (who is now a resurrected, celestial being) would match the description of the personage provided by the Lord—"holding the scepter of power in his hand, clothed with light for a covering, whose mouth shall utter words, eternal words; while his bowels shall be a fountain of truth." In 1905, the First Presidency of the Church (Joseph F. Smith, John R. Winder, and Anthon H. Lund)—though they considered the prophecy of Doctrine and Covenants 85 unfulfilled and closed due to repentance—allowed for the possibility that a bishop who would be called of God and sustained by the entire Church could yet carry out the duty once assigned to Bishop Edward Partridge in Zion.[5]

QUESTION 4

Is the Lord Jesus Christ currently aware of the exact time when the Second Coming will take place?

Answer:

In Mark 13, the Savior is quoted as saying that neither He nor the angels of heaven know the time of the Second Coming (see v. 32); that information, according to this passage, is known only to God the Father. But the corresponding verse in the Joseph Smith Translation of the Bible states that even though the angels of heaven do not know the day nor the hour of the Second Coming, there is no such restriction placed upon the Son of God (see JST, Mark 13:47). In 3 Nephi 12:48, it is revealed that after the Redeemer was resurrected, He informed the Nephites in the New World that He was then "perfect" like the God the Father. If Jesus Christ did not know the time of the Second Coming at that point, it would have been impossible for Him to claim perfection. Elder Bruce R. McConkie has taken the position that the Messiah indeed "knows the set time [of the Second Coming] and so does His Father."[6]

QUESTION 5

How do some Latter-day Saints interpret the "Second David" or "David of the Last Days" prophecy that is mentioned by such Old Testament prophets as Hosea, Jeremiah, and Ezekiel?

Answer:

It is not clear where the initial Latter-day Saint understanding of this prophecy originated, but several pieces of historical information may prove helpful in answering this question.

When the Prophet Joseph Smith dedicated the temple in Kirtland, Ohio, on March 27, 1836, he petitioned God the Father to redeem the city of Jerusalem and also to break off the yoke of bondage from the house of David—the house from whence originally came the kings of Israel (see D&C 109:62–63). A few years later Joseph Smith sent Orson Hyde to Jerusalem to dedicate that land as part of the program of restoration in the last days. When Elder Hyde offered the dedicatory prayer on October 24, 1841, he said to the Father: "Let [the powers of the earth] know that it is Thy good pleasure to restore the kingdom to Israel—raise up Jerusalem as its capital, and constitute her people a distinct nation and government, with David Thy servant, even a descendant from the loins of ancient David, to be their king."[7] It is not known if Joseph Smith had instructed Elder Hyde to make this reference in his prayer or whether Elder Hyde (who was of the lineage of Judah) was simply drawing inspiration from prophecies such as that found in Ezekiel 37:24–25.

The idea of a king named David ruling over Israel in the last days appears to have been fairly widespread in early LDS history. A Philadelphia-based periodical called the *Gospel Reflector* published an article on the Millennium that was reprinted in the *Times and Seasons* in Nauvoo on February 15, 1842. Apparently written by editors Erastus Snow and Benjamin Winchester, this article clearly refers to an Israelite king named David in the last days who would be "a literal descendant" of Israel's famed monarch of the same name. A king would be necessary because, according to the reasoning of the authors, it would be inconsistent to suppose that Jesus Christ would always be personally present on the earth during the Millennium. The article's authors made it plain, however, that this earthly king would be subject to Christ.[8]

From the sparse historical evidence on this subject, it seems clear that the Prophet Joseph Smith did indeed subscribe to the idea of a latter-day David. On July 27, 1842, the Prophet received a revelation from the Lord for Newel K. Whitney, which reads in part that "through the power of anointing David may reign king over Israel which shall hereafter be revealed."[9] And on March 10, 1844, only months before his death, the Prophet taught publicly that "the priesthood that [king David] received, and the throne and kingdom of David is to be taken from him and given to another by the name of David in the last days, raised up out of his lineage."[10]

In more modern times, another interpretation of the Old Testament prophecies of the latter-day David has been championed. Apostles such as Mark E. Peterson and Bruce R. McConkie have concluded that the figure foretold in ancient scripture is none other than the Lord Jesus Christ—who an angel of God declared would inherit "the throne of His father David" and reign over Israel forever (Luke 1:32–33). McConkie, speaking of what he termed "The Davidic Myth," writes:

> This wresting of the written word assumes that someone of prophetic stature will arise in the Church in the last days, to preside as a Second David, and to prepare the way before the second coming of the Son of Man. That there may be one or many brethren called David who preside over the Church in this dispensation is of no moment. The scriptures that speak of King David reigning in the last days are Messianic; they have reference to the millennial reign of the Lord Jesus Christ.[11]

Probably the safest and most reasonable stance to take on this issue is to hearken to what the Lord said to Newel K. Whitney through His duly authorized mouthpiece. He declared that more information on this subject "shall hereafter be revealed."

QUESTION 6

Will the Lamanites take the lead in building the city of New Jerusalem and its temple?

Answer:

After considering the evidence used to support this notion, President Joseph Fielding Smith made the following remarks:

> My attention has been called to statements in the Book of Mormon which some interpret to mean that the Lamanites will take the lead in building the temple and the New Jerusalem in Missouri. But I fail to find any single passage which indicates that this is to be the order of things when these great events are to be fulfilled.
>
> Most of the passages used as evidence, in an attempt to prove that the Lamanites will take the lead and we are to follow, seem to come from the instruction given by our Lord when He visited the Nephites after His resurrection. Chapters 20 and 21 of Third Nephi are the main sources for this conclusion. But I fail to find in any of the words delivered by our Savior any declaration out of which this conclusion can be reached. It all comes about by a misunderstanding and an improper interpretation.[12]

Bruce R. McConkie similarly offers thoughts about what he termed "The Lamanite-Temple Myth":

> An occasional whiff of nonsense goes around the Church acclaiming that the Lamanites will build the temple in the New Jerusalem and that Ephraim and others will come to their assistance. This illusion is born of an inordinate love for Father Lehi's children and of a desire to see them all become now as Samuel the Lamanite once was. The Book of Mormon passages upon which it is thought to rest have reference not to the Lamanites but to the whole house of Israel. The temple in Jackson County [Missouri] will be built by Ephraim, meaning the Church as it is now constituted; this is where the keys of temple building are vested, and it will be to this Ephraim that all the other tribes will come in due course to receive their temple blessings.[13]

While serving in the Quorum of the Twelve Apostles, Spencer W. Kimball expressed a similar view: "They, the Ten Tribes, you, the Lamanites, and the believing of us, also carrying the blood of Israel, will jointly build the city to our God, the New Jerusalem, with its magnificent temple."[14]

QUESTION 7

Didn't Brigham Young prophesy that before the Saints returned to Jackson County, Missouri, the western boundary of that state would be destroyed to such a degree that there wouldn't even be a yellow dog left to wag its tail?

Answer:

This claim, which calls for careful scrutiny, apparently first appeared among comments made by J. Golden Kimball during general conference in October 1930.[15] From the text of his remarks, it is clear that he was repeating information contained in a document, rather than reciting something that he had only heard. Thorough analysis reveals that this document contains statements Amanda H. Wilcox said she heard Heber C. Kimball make in May 1868. In the document, the so-called prophecy about the yellow dog is attributed by Heber C. Kimball, to President Brigham Young. Thus, the information presented by J. Golden Kimball can be described as third-hand at best.

However, it appears that this prophecy did not originate with Brigham Young either. An examination of the sermons of the Prophet Joseph Smith reveals that he made a comment on July 19, 1840 that is a close match to the "yellow dog prophecy." The Prophet reportedly said on that date: "I prophesy that the time shall be when these Saints shall ride proudly over the mountains of Missouri and no Gentile dog nor Missouri dog shall dare lift a tongue against them but will lick up the dust from beneath their feet. And I pray the Father that many here may realize this and see it with their eyes."[16]

The phrases "Gentile dog" and "Missouri dog" in this passage are obviously meant to be understood as figurative references to people who oppressed the Saints when they resided in Jackson County, Missouri. Some LDS scholars have thus interpreted the "yellow dog" comment made by Brigham Young as a reference to "a persecuting gentile settler."[17]

Sometimes another prophecy uttered by Joseph Smith—one about Zion being swept clean—is tied together with the yellow-dog prediction. One LDS scholar, however, has cautioned that these are two separate events that should not be combined. Instead, it should be remembered that the area of the future Zion was indeed swept clean during the Civil War era—and thus the "clean sweep prophecy" has already been fulfilled.[18]

QUESTION 8

Is there any way to turn aside the terrible judgments that are predicted to be poured out upon the earth's inhabitants during the last days?

Answer:
An examination of Doctrine and Covenants 39 suggests that in specific cases the judgments of the Lord can indeed be staid. Nevertheless, it does not appear that God's judgments will be nullified as far as what He has decreed for the entire earth.

> Behold, verily, verily, I say unto you, that the people in Ohio call upon me in much faith, thinking I will *stay my hand in judgment upon the nations,* but *I cannot deny my word.*
>
> Wherefore lay to with your might and call faithful laborers into my vineyard, that it may be pruned for the last time.
>
> And *inasmuch as they do repent and receive the fullness of my gospel, and become sanctified, I will stay mine hand in judgment.* (v. 16–18; emphasis added)

This same principle can be seen in the story of the Old Testament city of Nineveh; the people repented of their evil deeds and did not perish; the Lord's fierce anger was "turned away" from them (JST, Jonah 3:1–10). Perhaps this is the context that best explains the passage in Doctrine and Covenants 84:96–97, which states in relation to the last days, "For I, the Almighty, have laid my hands upon the nations, to scourge them for their wickedness. And plagues shall go forth, and they shall not be taken from the earth until I have completed my work, which shall be *cut short in righteousness*" (emphasis added).

It appears, then, that the work of divine destruction among the nations of the earth will go forward because the Lord has proclaimed that such will take place, and His word cannot return unto Him void (see Isa. 55:11). But if people in a certain location choose to repent of their wicked ways and accept the Lord's message of redemption, His work will be "cut short" or halted among them because they have turned unto "righteousness."

QUESTION 9

Hasn't it been prophesied that the Latter-day Saints will have to walk back to Jackson County, Missouri, when the time comes to return there and build up the city of Zion?

Answer:

The seed of this myth seems to have been planted by a statement President Joseph F. Smith made on December 3, 1882. During a discourse he delivered in the Provo, Utah, tabernacle, he asked the question, "When God leads the people back to Jackson County [Missouri], how will He do it?" He responded by offering the following thoughts.

> Let me picture to you how some of us *may* be gathered and led to Jackson County. *I think* I see two or three hundred thousand people wending their way across the great plain enduring the nameless hardships of the journey, herding and guarding their cattle by day and by night, and defending themselves and [their] little ones from foes on the right hand and on the left, as when they came here. They will find the journey back to Jackson County will be as real as when they came out here. Now, mark it. And though you may be led by the power of God "with a stretched out arm," it will not be more manifest than the leading [of] the people out here to those [who] participate in it. They will think there are a great many hardships to endure in this manifestation of the power of God, and it will be left, *perhaps* to their children to see the glory of their deliverance, just as it is left for us to see the glory of our former deliverance from the hands of those [who] sought to destroy us. *This is one way to*

> *look at it*. It is certainly *a practical view*. Some might ask, what will become of the railroads? *I fear* that the sifting process would be insufficient were we to travel by railroads (emphasis added).[19]

When all of the qualifying phrases in this paragraph are taken into consideration, President Smith appears not to have been relaying a heaven-sent prophecy to his audience but rather to have simply offered his own personal opinion.

QUESTION 10

Wasn't there a prophecy uttered by a Catholic monk in 1739 that foretold of the restoration of the true Church within one hundred years?

Answer:

The story of this alleged prophecy first appeared in an LDS Church periodical near the end of the nineteenth century. Jacob Spori, a Swiss convert to the Church in 1877, wrote of the prophecy for the *Juvenile Instructor* in 1893. He claimed that a book called *Hope of Zion*—written in German by one Lutius Gratianus and published in Basel, Switzerland, in 1739—contained a detailed prophecy about the restoration of the true Church before the Second Coming of Jesus Christ and within 100 years of this prophecy's utterance. Parts of the prophecy allegedly referred to a persecuted people who lived by a great lake and who would build a magnificent temple. These people would send missionaries out into the world and they would have priesthood offices such as prophets, Apostles, elders, teachers, and deacons.[20]

In reality, a book called *Hope of Zion* was indeed published, but it came forth in Bern, Switzerland, in 1732, in the German language and was attributed to Christophilus Gratianus. This book was reissued in an expanded form in 1737 at Basel, Switzerland, under the name of the same author. A 1739 edition of this book was never issued. Christophilus Gratianus was actually an alias for

Samuel Lutz, a preacher of the Protestant Swiss Reformed Church. The name Lutius Gratianus never appears on any of the works written by Samuel Lutz but seems to be a combination of Lutz's latinized name (Samuel *Lucius*) and his pseudonym (Christophilus *Gatianus*). For some unknown reason, this person was further transfigured into "Lutius Gratus," the Catholic priest.[21]

The information presented in Spori's 1893 *Juvenile Instructor* article seems to be the product of a faulty memory. When Oskar K. Winters (secretary of the Swiss-German mission in 1922) read through the 1732 edition of *Hope of Zion,* he noted that it was "rich in prophecies concerning the restoration of the gospel and is remarkable in that it mentions a church with prophets and patriarchs and that the Urim and Thummim would be restored, etc." But he failed to find the elements of the "prophecy" as remembered by Spori. Winters surmised that perhaps the Spori prophecy represents his own synopsis or summary of elements that were scattered throughout the book.

Rulon S. Wells of the First Quorum of the Seventy concluded after reading the volume under discussion in 1897 that the "prophecy" was bogus. He even wrote an article called "A Fraudulent Prophecy Exposed" for the *Improvement Era.* And he said that he hoped that this 'prophecy' would not be used either at home or in the mission field as a means of support for "the great work of the Master."[22]

QUESTION 11

Hasn't it been prophesied that all of the mountains of the earth will be melted or vanish away when the Second Coming occurs?

Answer:

A portion of Doctrine and Covenants 133 reads as follows:

> [The prayer will be uttered:] "O that thou wouldst rend the heavens, that thou wouldst come down, that the mountains might flow down at Thy presence."

> And it shall be answered upon their heads; for the presence of the Lord shall be as the melting fire that burneth, and as the fire which causeth the waters to boil.
>
> O Lord, thou shalt come down to make Thy name known to Thine adversaries, and all nations shall tremble at Thy presence—
>
> When thou doest terrible things, things they look not for;
>
> Yea, when thou comest down, and the mountains flow down at Thy presence, Thou shalt meet him who rejoiceth and worketh righteousness, who remembereth Thee in Thy ways. (v. 40–44)

A comparison of this modern canonical text with Isaiah 64:1–5 shows that the Doctrine and Covenants text is a definite parallel. The prophet Isaiah says:

> Oh that Thou wouldest rend the heavens, that Thou wouldest come down, that the mountains might flow down at Thy presence,
>
> As when the melting fire burneth, the fire causeth the waters to boil, to make Thy name known to Thine adversaries, that the nations may tremble at Thy presence!
>
> When Thou didst terrible things which we looked not for, Thou camest down, the mountains flowed down at Thy presence.
>
> For since the beginning of the world men have not heard, nor perceived by the ear, neither hath the eye seen, O God, beside Thee, what He hath prepared for him that waiteth for Him.
>
> Thou meetest him that rejoiceth and worketh righteousness, those that remember Thee in Thy ways.

Clearly, the Lord is citing the Isaiah passage in the Doctrine and Covenants, but the key to understanding the remark about the mountains is found in the Hebrew words that underlie Isaiah's text. In Isaiah 64:1 the phrase "flow down" is translated from the single Hebrew word *zalal,* which means "shake" or "quake." The same applies to the phrase "flowed down" in verse 3. If this is taken into consideration, and if the passage is reread with the objective of comparing the imagery of verses 1 and 2, then it becomes apparent that the mountains quake at the presence of Jehovah, and His adversaries do the same. The mention of fire that melts and causes water to boil, in verse 2, may simply be a reference to ancient Israelite imagery that describes God as "a consuming fire" (Deut. 4:24; 9:3; Heb. 12:29).

Doctrine and Covenants 133:22 also speaks of the voice of the Lord breaking down the mountains. If the text of this entire verse and the preceding verse is taken into account, however, it becomes clear that this is not a reference to the literal destruction of mountains but is rather a description of the power of the Lord's voice. It is as the voice of many waters and as the voice of great thunder; it is strong enough to break down mountains and to make valleys vanish away.

Section 109 of the Doctrine and Covenants also contains a reference to the mountains "flow[ing] down" at the presence of the Lord (v. 74). This section of modern canonical writings is the dedicatory prayer of the Kirtland Temple. Since historical documents reveal that this prayer was written by a committee—which drew heavily upon Old Testament scriptures[23]—the reference to the mountains flowing down can probably best be understood as representing the heartfelt desire of the prayer's authors to have the prophecies of the last days fulfilled.

In another scriptural text, the Lord admonishes His Saints to "continue in steadfastness, looking forth for the heavens to be shaken, and the earth to tremble and to reel to and fro as a drunken man, and for the valleys to be exalted, and for the mountains to be made low, and for the rough places to become smooth—and all this when the angel shall sound his trumpet" (D&C 49:23). In this passage it appears that the Lord has stitched together imagery from three separate verses found in the book of Isaiah. First is Isaiah 13:13. "Therefore I will shake the heavens, and the earth shall remove out of her place, in the wrath of the Lord of hosts, and in the day of His fierce anger." Following that is Isaiah 24:20: "The earth shall reel to and fro like a drunkard." And the final reference mentions the mountains: "Every valley shall be exalted, and every mountain and hill shall be made low: and the crooked shall be made straight, and the rough places plain" (Isa. 40:4).

Notice that even though Isaiah 40:4 says that "every" mountain and hill will be made low, the corresponding text in the Doctrine and Covenants does not; it says only that "the mountains" will be made low. A related text in the book of Revelation says that "the mountains" will not be found (16:20; cf. Hel. 14:23). The context of this passage is critical to understanding the whole issue of the disappearing mountains. The text of Revelation 16:16–20 teaches that during the battle of Armageddon there will be an earthquake of colossal magnitude, mightier than any earthquake that has occurred since man has inhabited the earth. Ezekiel, in chapters 38 and 39 of his book, discusses the battle of Gog/Magog (the battle of Armageddon); he says, "There shall be *a great shaking in the land of Israel*" so that the fish, birds, beasts, and humans will shake at the Lord's presence and the mountains will be broken in pieces (emphasis added; see Appendix 3). The prophet Zechariah adds the final bit of clarification regarding this issue, saying that when the Lord touches His feet on the Mount of Olives, the mountain will break in two pieces, and from Geba to Rimmon (south of Jerusalem), all the land shall be turned into a plain and lifted up (see Appendix 3). In other words, the "disappearing mountains" will be a local event, not a worldwide cataclysm.

QUESTION 12

How should Latter-day Saints react to the great upheavals and terrible situations that will inevitably occur during the last days?

Answer:

Some Latter-day Saints believe that the catastrophes of the last days are inevitable and that they can do nothing to make a difference when they occur. Glen L. Pace—counselor in the Presiding Bishopric—teaches otherwise. He submits that people with this kind of attitude need an adjustment in their way of thinking. His first recommends overcoming the perspective of fatalism.

> We know the prophecies of the future. We know the final outcome. We know the world collectively will not repent and consequently the last days will be filled with much pain and suffering. Therefore, we could throw up our hands and do nothing but pray for the end to come so the millennial reign could begin. To do so would forfeit our right to participate in the grand event we are all awaiting. We must all become players in the winding-up scene, not spectators. We must do all we can to prevent calamities, and then do everything possible to assist and comfort the victims of tragedies that do occur. . . .
>
> As we . . . fight the war of good against evil, light against darkness, and truth against falsehood, we must not neglect our responsibility of dressing the wounds of those who have fallen in battle. There is no room in the kingdom for fatalism.
>
> The second attitude adjustment is to not allow ourselves to find satisfaction in calamities of the last days. Sometimes we tend to take joy in seeing the

> natural consequences of sin unfold. We might feel some vindication for being ignored by most of the world and persecuted and berated by others. When we see earthquakes, wars, famines, disease, poverty, and heartbreak, we may be tempted to say, "Well, we warned them. We told them a thousand times not to engage in those activities."

Bishop Pace points to the speech of King Benjamin in the Book of Mormon and admonishes the Saints to heed his counsel. The king said, "Perhaps thou shalt say: The man has brought upon himself his misery; therefore I will stay my hand, and will not give unto him of my food, nor impart unto him of my substance that he may not suffer, for his punishments are just—But I say unto you, O man, whosoever doeth this the same hath great cause to repent" (Mosiah 4:17–18).[24]

QUESTION 13

What is the "White-Horse" prophecy and what have LDS Church leaders said about it?

Answer:

The so-called White-Horse prophecy was reportedly uttered by Joseph Smith at his home in Nauvoo, Illinois, on May 7, 1843. Two Latter-day Saints (Edwin Rushton and Theodore Turley)[25] attested that they were standing directly before the Church leader when this prediction of the future was spoken. They also claimed that at least part of the information relayed by President Smith was being shown to him in a vision while he spoke.

This alleged prophecy was couched in the language of a parable, drawing directly upon imagery found in the book of Revelation. It was essentially about the future of the Saints (the White Horse) and said, in part, that the Lord's people would suffer legislative persecution at the hands of the U.S. government but that they would also become a very wealthy group in the midst of the Rocky Mountains. This prophecy spoke of a revolution that would take place in the land of America during a time when wickedness and crime would be rampant and the government would fail. Conditions would supposedly became so alarming that Gentiles would flock to the Rocky Mountains in order to live among a righteous people, even though they would not desire to convert to the LDS faith. There would reportedly be a war with an inhuman amount of bloodshed, and in the process the United States would be broken up and no reasonable form of government would exist. Foreign powers would intervene in the troubles of the beleaguered country but they would be considered "invaders" by some. The White Horse and Red Horse are called "Guardians" in this foretelling of latter-day events; the White Horse and Red Horse (perhaps the British) would, in some unspecified manner, support the United States Constitution. It would be in these days, the prophecy averred, that the Lord would set up His millennial kingdom.

There are elements of this prophecy that nineteenth-century Church leaders accepted without question as originating with Joseph Smith (see question 16 below), while other aspects of it clearly did not meet with their approval. In October 1918 general conference, a strong negative response was directed toward the White-Horse prophecy. Joseph Fielding Smith, objecting to it on administrative grounds, said from the pulpit:

> I have discovered that people have copies of a purported vision by the Prophet Joseph Smith given in Nauvoo, and some people are circulating this supposed vision, or revelation, or conversation which the prophet is reported to have held with a number of individuals in the city of Nauvoo. I want to say to you, my brethren and sisters, that if you understand the Church articles and covenants, if

> you will read the scriptures and become familiar with those things which are recorded in the revelations from the Lord, it will not be necessary for you to ask any questions in regard to the authenticity or otherwise of any purported revelation, vision, or manifestation that proceeds out of darkness, concocted in some corner, surreptitiously presented, and not coming through the proper channels of the Church. Let me add that when a revelation comes for the guidance of this people, you may be sure that it will not be presented in some mysterious manner contrary to the order of the Church. It will go forth in such form that the people will understand that it comes from those who are in authority, for it will be sent either to the presidents of stakes and the bishops of the wards over the signatures of the presiding authorities, or it will be published in some of the regular papers or magazines under the control and direction of the Church or it will be presented before such a gathering as this, at a general conference. It will not spring up in some distant part of the Church and be in the hands of some obscure individual without authority, and thus be circulated among the Latter-day Saints. Now, you may remember this.[26]

The remarks of President Joseph F. Smith followed immediately after those of his Apostle-son. He left no doubt about his feelings toward this alleged prophecy:

> The ridiculous story about the "red horse," and "the black horse," and "the white horse," and a lot of trash that has been circulated about and printed and sent around as a great revelation given by the

> Prophet Joseph Smith, is a matter that was gotten up, I understand, some ten years after the death of the Prophet Joseph Smith, by two of our brethren who put together some broken sentences from the Prophet that they may have heard him utter from time to time, and formulated this so-called revelation out of it, and it was never spoken by the Prophet in the manner in which they have put it forth. It is simply false; that is all there is to it. . . .
>
> Now, these stories of revelations that are being circulated around are of no consequence except for rumor and silly talk by persons that have no authority. The fact of the matter is simply here and this. No man can enter into God's rest unless he will absorb the truth insofar that all error, all falsehood, all misunderstandings and misstatements he will be able to sift thoroughly and dissolve, and know that it is error and not truth. When you know God's truth, when you enter into God's rest, you will not be hunting after revelations from Tom, Dick and Harry all over the world. You will not be following the will of the wisps of the vagaries of men and women who advance nonsense and their own ideas. When you know the truth, you will abide in the truth, and the truth will make you free, and it is only the truth that will free you from the errors of men, and from the falsehood and misrepresentations of the evil one who lies in wait to deceive and to mislead the people of God from the paths of righteousness and truth.[27]

Bruce R. McConkie accepts the views of his leadership predecessors, calling the White-Horse prophecy a "false and deceptive" document. And he chastises the Saints for being so intensely interested in "supposed prophetic utterances" while at the same time paying less attention to the voluminous verified prophecies found within the scriptures.[28]

QUESTION 14

Isn't there a lengthy vision about the last days recorded in Wilford Woodruff's journal, and wasn't this manifestation experienced by some General Authority?

Answer:

Indeed, Wilford Woodruff's journal contains the description of a vision about the last days. It describes terrible calamities in the future, as well as the return of the Latter-day Saints to Jackson County in the state of Missouri. This vision occurred on December 16, 1877, but Elder Woodruff referred to it as "very strange." Although the name of the visionary was never recorded in the Apostle's journal, a blank spot was left, apparently to be filled in at a later time. In combination, these facts indicate that Elder Woodruff did not experience this spiritual manifestation himself. John Taylor is the person most often associated with this vision, because the experiencer mentioned reading the scriptures in French just before the vision occurred, and Elder Taylor spoke the French language. However, Elder Taylor's knowledge of French was limited, and it would seem logical that Wilford Woodruff would have known if a fellow Apostle had been the one who saw this vision. Another Church leader who has been suggested as the recipient of this manifestation is Joseph F. Smith. But in an article published in the Deseret Evening News on November 17, 1880, he denied being the person in question and declared, "I never knew but two or three words in French."[29] It is difficult to understand the full context, or even judge the veracity, of this vision without knowing who actually received it.

QUESTION 15

Where are the lost ten tribes of Israel and in what manner will they return in the last days?

Answer:

The tenth Article of Faith states that Latter-day Saints "believe in the literal gathering of Israel and in the restoration of the ten tribes." On April 3, 1836, Joseph Smith and Oliver Cowdery jointly received—from the resurrected prophet Moses—"the keys of the gathering of Israel from the four parts of the earth, and the leading of the ten tribes from the land of the north" (D&C 110:11).

The lost ten tribes are commonly referred to as being in "the north country" (Jer. 31:8) because they were initially transported north of the nation of Israel when they were taken captive by the Assyrians more than seven hundred years before the birth of Christ. In Zechariah 2:6, the Lord indicates that for the Israelites to be in "the land of the north" is akin to saying that they have been "spread . . . abroad as the four winds of the heaven" or to the four directions of the compass (north, south, east, and west). The sayings of the prophet Nephi in the Book of Mormon agree with this view. In 1 Nephi 22:3–5, this early Israelite prophet enlightens his brethren about the "lost" tribes of Israel, specifying that they have been "scattered to and fro" upon the earth and their exact location is unknown to man. Indeed, Doctrine and Covenants 133:26 acknowledges that those Israelites who are "in the north" are not confined to one location but are rather scattered throughout a variety of "countries."

The clear implication of the Lord's declaration in Jeremiah 16:15–16 is that the children of Israel who are scattered among "all the lands" of the earth, and even those who are in "the land of the north," will be gathered back by missionaries whom the Lord Himself will send out after them. In 3 Nephi 21:20–29, the words of the Savior follow these ideas closely. There the Redeemer foretells the work of His Father among "the tribes which have been lost," and He stipulates that this work includes the preaching of the gospel to the dispersed of Israel—the purpose being that they might come unto the Son of God and call upon the Father in His name.

Elder Bruce R. McConkie's stance on the whereabouts of the lost ten tribes is in accord with the scriptures cited above. He teaches that these members of the house of Israel are "scattered in all nations of the earth, primarily in the nations north of the lands of their first inheritance." And, he adds, they "are to come back like anyone else: by accepting the Book of Mormon and believing the restored gospel."[30]

QUESTION 16

Did Joseph Smith prophesy that the Constitution of the United States would someday hang by a thread and then be saved by the elders of the Church?

Answer:

The first statement by the Prophet Joseph Smith on this subject was apparently made on July 19, 1840—several months after he had returned from a trip to Washington, D.C., where he discovered that even the president of the United States would not protect the Saints in their Constitutionally guaranteed rights. Two different sets of notes relate the Prophet's remarks on this occasion. The first set of notes, made almost exactly six months after the fact, was recorded by Orson Pratt, relaying information he had learned in November 1840 from his brother Parley. The elements of the Prophet's talk, as recalled by the Pratts, run in sequence as follows: Zion is all of North and South America. The twelve olive trees are twelve stakes. Jackson County, Missouri, is the center. The government is fallen and needs redeeming. It is guilty of blood and cannot stand as it now is but will become so near desolation as to hang as it were by a single hair. Then the servants go to the nations of the earth and gather the strength of the Lord's house—a mighty army. And this is the redemption of Zion. The Saints shall have redeemed that government and reinstated it in all its purity and glory, that America may be an asylum for the remnants of all nations.[31]

In summary, it can be said that the Prophet believed that (1) the government is fallen, (2) the government will come so near desolation that it will be like it is hanging by a single hair, (3) the Saints will redeem the government to its former purity and glory, and (4) this redemption will be accomplished in connection with the gathering of Israel from all the nations of the earth.

The second set of notes on the Prophet's discourse dated July 19, 1840, is found in the Howard and Martha Coray Notebook. These notes seem to have been written no earlier than September 5, 1854.[32] Nevertheless, the elements found in the Coray report closely match with the Pratt reminiscence. The relevant elements of the Coray report include the following: The land of Zion consists of all of North and South America. The twelve olive trees are twelve stakes. The twelve stakes must be built up before the redemption of Zion can take place. The nations of the earth will be at war while the twelve stakes are being built, but the Saints will be at peace during this same period. When the Lord's servants are building the watchtower of Zion, the enemy will scatter the seed of the twelve olive trees abroad. The scattered seed will "wake up the nations of the whole earth." Then the Lord will call upon His servants to come and fight His battle in the land of His vineyard. The rulers of the earth and the Saints in foreign countries will come and "fight for the land of [the Lord's] vineyard." The Saints may plead at the feet of magistrates, judges, governors, senators, and presidents for a long time, but to no avail. The Saints will find no favor in the courts of the present government. This nation will be on the very verge of crumbling to pieces and tumbling to the ground; and when the Constitution is upon the brink of ruin, this people will be the staff upon which the nation shall lean and they shall bear the Constitution away from the very verge of destruction.[33]

A careful comparison of the Pratt and Coray notes with section 101 of the Doctrine and Covenants (received on December 16, 1833) reveals that Joseph Smith's remarks on July 19, 1840 were heavily influenced by the content of that revelation. In that scripture the Lord speaks of the "stakes" of Zion (v. 21) and teaches in parable form "concerning the redemption of Zion" (v. 43). He speaks of a vineyard situated on a choice piece of land (see v. 44), a command given to the servants of a nobleman to plant twelve olive trees (see v. 44), a command to build a watchtower (see v. 45), the scattering of the servants by an enemy (see v. 51), and the call of the nobleman to gather "warriors" in order to rout the enemy (see v. 54–57). The Lord also states in Doctrine and Covenants 101 that it is His will that the Saints "importune for redress, and redemption, by the hands of those who are placed as *rulers* and are in authority . . . according to the laws and *constitution* of the people" which He Himself had suffered to be established (v. 76–77, 80; emphasis added). The Lord then foretells, or prophesies, that if the Saints petition the judge, governor, and president on this matter and their petition goes unheeded then, "in His time," the Lord will "cut off" the unjust stewards and "vex the nation" in His fury (v. 85–90). Nevertheless, this prophecy was conditional, and these dire consequences could be avoided (see v. 92).

Another time the Prophet evidently referred to the Constitution as being in danger was on May 6, 1843, during a parade of the Nauvoo Legion. With a general of the United States Army and some of his staff present, the Prophet reportedly spoke on "the Constitution and government of the United States stating that the time would come when the Constitution and government would hang by a brittle thread and would be ready to fall into other hands but this people the Latter day Saints will step forth and save it."[34]

Just a few days later—on May 18, 1843—the Prophet conversed with one of those individuals listed in the Lord's prophetic warning of 1833, a judge named Stephen A. Douglas. Joseph Smith said to him:

> I prophesy in the name of the Lord God of Israel, unless the United States redress[es] the wrongs committed upon the Saints in the state of Missouri and punish[es] the crimes committed by her officers that in a few years the government will be utterly overthrown and wasted, and there will not be so much as a potsherd left, for their wickedness in permitting the murder of men, women and children, and the wholesale plunder and extermination of thousands of her citizens to go unpunished, thereby perpetrating a foul and corroding blot upon the fair fame of this great republic, the very thought of which would have caused the high-minded and patriotic framers of the Constitution of the United States to hide their faces with shame.[35]

Just seven months later (December 16, 1843), Joseph Smith returned to this theme. As he signed an official petition to the United States Congress for redress of losses suffered by the Saints during the Missouri persecution, he "prophesied" to those assembled saying, "by virtue of the holy Priesthood vested in me, and in the name of the Lord Jesus Christ . . . if Congress will not hear our petition and grant us protection, they shall be broken up as a government."[36] Concerning this, Brigham H. Roberts states:

> This prediction doubtless has reference to the party in power; to the "government" considered as the administration; not to the "government" considered as the country; but the administration party, the Democratic Party, which had controlled the destiny of the country for forty years. It is matter of

> history that [a] few years later the party then in power lost control of the national government, followed by the terrible conflict of the Civil War. The party against which the above prediction was made so far lost its influence that it did not again return to power for a quarter of a century; and when it did return to power it was with such modified views as to many great questions of government, that it could scarcely be regarded as the same party except in name.
>
> Lest it should be urged that the Whig party was in control of the government in 1843, I call attention to the fact that while General Harrison, a Whig, was elected in 1840, he was President only one month, as he died on the 4th of April, 1841. His whole cabinet, excepting Mr. Webster, Secretary of State, resigned, and the Vice President became President. Though elected by the Whigs Mr. Tyler was a Democrat "and the Whig administration had but a month's actual existence" (Morris, *History of the United States,* 311–12).[37]

With Elder Roberts pointing to the possibility that at least parts of Joseph Smith's utterances were fulfilled in the 1860s, it seems appropriate to mention that on March 29, 1887, two members of the First Presidency of the Church (John Taylor and George Q. Cannon) suggested the following to Erastus Snow, one of the members of the Quorum of the Twelve Apostles: "It would appear that we have reached that era in our history, so long since foretold, when the Constitution of the United States would hang by a single thread and the elders of Israel alone would contend for its preservation."[38]

Notes to Chapter 6

1. Bruce R. McConkie, "To the Koreans, and All the People of Asia," Address to Returned Missionaries, 5 Mar. 1971, Provo, Utah, quoted in Spencer J. Palmer, *The Expanding Church* (Salt Lake City: Deseret Book, 1978), 142.

2. *HC* 1:297–99.

3. See ibid., 2:302–3.

4. Letter, William W. Phelps to Brigham Young, 6 May 1867, LDS Church Archives, Salt Lake City, Utah.

5. *MFP*, 4:108–20. Long after the death of Bishop Edward Partridge, Elder Orson Pratt (after quoting D&C 85:7) said that he still looked forward to the time when the Lord would send a person "ordained to [the] purpose" of assigning inheritances in Zion (*JD*, 12:323).

6. *The Millennial Messiah*, 27.

7. *HC* 4:457.

8. *T&S*, vol. 3, no. 8, 15 Feb. 1842, 690.

9. *The Essential Joseph Smith* (Salt Lake City: Signature Books, 1995), 166.

10. *HC* 6:253.

11. *NWAF*, 518. For further reading on this topic, see Kent P. Jackson, "The Latter-day David," in Kent P. Jackson, *Lost Tribes and Last Days* (Salt Lake City: Deseret Book, 2005), 107–11; Mark E. Peterson, "A Final King David," in Mark E. Peterson, *Joseph of Egypt* (Salt Lake City: Deseret Book, 1981), 66–68; Bruce D. Porter, comments in FARMS Review of Books, vol. 4, 1992, 43–49; Victor L. Ludlow, "David, Prophetic Figure of Last Days," in *EM*, 1:360–61; Daniel H. Ludlow, references in *Nurturing Faith Through the Book of Mormon* (Salt Lake City: Deseret Book, 1995), 77–78; Hoyt W. Brewster Jr., *Doctrine and Covenants Encyclopedia* (Salt Lake City: Bookcraft, 1988), 255; Rodney Turner, "The Two Davids," in Richard D. Draper, ed., *A Witness of Jesus Christ* (Salt Lake City: Deseret Book, 1990), 240–60; Sydney B. Sperry, *The*

Voice of Israel's Prophets (Salt Lake City: Deseret Book, 1952), 129–30, 177, 414; Victor L. Ludlow, *Isaiah: Prophet, Seer, and Poet* (Salt Lake City: Deseret Book, 1982), 168–70; Victor L. Ludlow, *Unlocking the Old Testament* (Salt Lake City: Deseret Book, 1981), 155–57; *The Millennial Messiah,* 602–11.

12. *DS,* 2:247–48.

13. *NWAF,* 519.

14. CR, Oct. 1959, 61.

15. See ibid., Oct. 1930, 59.

16. *WJS,* 418. It should be noted that this is not a prophecy uttered in the name of the Lord.

17. Ibid., 420, note 13.

18. See Monte S. Nyman, "When Will Zion be Redeemed?" in Leon R. Hartshorn, Dennis A. Wright, and Craig J. Ostler, ed., *The Doctrine and Covenants: A Book of Answers* (Salt Lake City: Deseret Book, 1996), 148. For more information on this topic, see *CHC* 533–59.

19. *JD,* 24:156–57.

20. See Jacob Spori, "True and False Theosophy," *Juvenile Instructor,* vol. 28, no. 21, 1 Nov. 1893, 672–74. A convenient overview of this subject can be found in Paul B. Pixton, "'Play it Again Sam': The Remarkable 'Prophecy' of Samuel Lutz, Alias Christophilus Gratianus, Reconsidered," *Brigham Young University Studies,* vol. 25, no. 3, Summer 1985, 27–46.

21. The transformation to Catholic priest reportedly took place when Thomas K. Marston first published his booklet entitled *Missionary Pal.*

22. Rulon S. Wells, "A Fraudulent Prophecy Exposed," *IE,* vol. 11, no. 3, Jan. 1908, 161–64.

23. See Matthew B. Brown and Paul Thomas Smith, *Symbols in Stone: Symbolism on the Early Temples of the Restoration* (American Fork, UT: Covenant, 1997), 49–50, 78, notes 30–32.

24. *Ensign,* Nov. 1990, 8–9.

25. See Frank Esshom, *Pioneers and Prominent Men of Utah*

(Salt Lake City: Utah Pioneers Book Publishing Co., 1913), 2:1145, 1218.

26. CR, Oct. 1918, 55.

27. Ibid., 57–58.

28. *MD,* 835.

29. See Richard E. Turley Jr., *Victims: The LDS Church and the Mark Hofmann Forgeries Case* (Urbana and Chicago: University of Illinois Press, 1992), 16–17, 19–20, 402, note 31, 403, note 33.

30. *NWAF,* 520. For further reading see Paul K. Browning, "Gathering Scattered Israel: Then and Now," *Ensign,* July 1998, 54–61.

31. Letter, Orson Pratt to George A. Smith, 21 Jan. 1841, Orson Pratt Papers, LDS Church Archives, Salt Lake City, Utah, cited in *Brigham Young University Studies,* vol. 21, no. 4, Fall 1981, 533.

32. See note 1 for the July 19, 1840 discourse in the revised edition of *The Words of Joseph Smith.*

33. See *Brigham Young University Studies,* vol. 19, no. 3, Spring 1979, 392–93.

34. *WJS,* 279, note 1.

35. *HC* 5:394.

36. Ibid., 6:116.

37. Ibid., footnote.

38. Letter, Presidents John Taylor and George Q. Cannon to Elder Erastus Snow, First Presidency Letterpress Copy Books, 29 Mar. 1887 (letter about the anticipation of raids being conducted under the provisions of the Edmunds-Tucker Act), cited in Samuel W. Taylor and Raymond W. Taylor, *The John Taylor Papers: Records of the Last Utah Pioneer* (Redwood City, CA: Taylor, 1985), 2:464. For further reading and sources that rehearse the Prophet's comments on the Constitution, see Larry E. Dahl and Donald Q. Cannon, ed., *Encyclopedia of Joseph Smith's Teachings* (Salt Lake City: Bookcraft, 1997), 143–46; D. Michael Stewart, "What do we know about the purported statement of Joseph Smith that the

Constitution would hang by a thread and that the Elders would save it?" *Ensign*, June 1976, 64–65; Preston Nibley, "What of Joseph Smith's Prophecy That the Constitution Would Hang by a Thread?" *Church News,* 15 Dec. 1948, 24.

APPENDIX 1

MORONI'S SCRIPTURE QUOTATIONS

When the angel Moroni appeared to Joseph Smith for the first time on September 22, 1823, the heavenly being spent many hours reciting a series of biblical scriptures and explaining how they related to the events of the dispensation of the fulness of times. It was so important that Joseph learn of these events that Moroni recounted the scripture set three separate times.

In Joseph Smith's published history, he mentions only a few of the numerous scriptures presented by the angel.[1] Fortunately, Oliver Cowdery spoke with the Prophet about his otherworldly visitation and then printed more of the details regarding Moroni's words.[2] This appendix provides a list of nearly all the scriptures Moroni used in his teaching of the young Prophet, according to Cowdery. A summary of their content then explains how they are related to the signs of the times, the Second Coming, and the Millennium.

In some instances in this appendix, the parameters of the scriptures noted by Oliver Cowdery have been expanded so that the full context of the message or themes can be more easily discerned.

The scriptures quoted by the angel Moroni were not necessarily presented to the Prophet in the same order as they are here.

Deuteronomy 32:[15–]**24.** Forsaking God and provoking Him with abominations; divine fire is to consume the earth, even the foundations of the mountains; the people will be brought to destruction.

Deuteronomy 32:43. God will "avenge the blood of His servants, and will render vengeance to His adversaries" (cf. Rev. 6:9–10).

Psalm 107:1–7. The Lord gathers His people from the four quarters of the earth and leads them to "a city of habitation" (i.e., Zion; cf. Ps. 132:13).

Psalm 146:10. The Lord God of Zion will "reign forever."

Isaiah 1:7, [21–27]. Zion is overthrown. Zion is in a state of apostasy. Zion will be redeemed and restored by God.

Isaiah 2:2–4. The temple will be established in the mountains during the last days and all nations will flow unto it. People will go there to learn the ways of the Lord, for His law will go forth from Zion and His word will go forth from Jerusalem. The Lord will judge and rebuke the nations. War will not be learned anymore.

Isaiah 4:[4]–6. Filth and blood will be removed by the spirit of judgment and burning. Dwellings on "mount Zion" will be overshadowed and protected by a cloud during the day and flaming fire at night.

Isaiah 11:[6–]16. There will be no enmity between animals; there will be no enmity between animals and man. The earth will be full of the knowledge of the Lord as the waters cover the sea. The Lord will set His hand the second time to recover the remnant of His people; He will gather them from the four corners of the earth. A "highway" created by God through the water will be used by the remnant of Israel to return. There will no longer be animosity between the tribes of Israel, and the adversaries of Judah will be cut off.

Isaiah 29:[10–]14. The prophets and seers of Israel have been covered by the Lord; they sleep; they do not see nor reveal. A sealed book is delivered to a person who is not learned and he is asked to read it. The Lord says that His people draw near to Him with their mouths and honor Him with their lips but their hearts are far from Him; their fear toward Him is taught by the precepts of men. Therefore the Lord will do a marvelous work and a wonder among His people. By this work the wisdom of the wise will perish and the understanding of the prudent will be hid.

Isaiah 43:[5–]6. The Lord will gather His sons and daughters from the ends of the earth.

Jeremiah 16:[14–]16. The Lord will gather the children of Israel by sending out "many fishers" and "many hunters" (i.e., missionaries).

Jeremiah 30:18–21. Jerusalem will be rebuilt. Israel will govern itself. Israel's oppressors will be punished.

Jeremiah 31:1, 6, 8–9, 27–28, 31–33. The Lord will "bring [the remnants of Israel] from the north country" (i.e., gather the lost ten tribes). The Lord will make a new covenant with the house of Israel. There will be acknowledgment between God and the families of Israel, the two parties of the covenant relationship. There will be a day when the cry will go out—"let us go up to Zion unto the Lord our God" (i.e., go to the temple).

Jeremiah 50:4–5. The children of Israel will ask the way to Zion and will desire to join themselves to the Lord in a perpetual covenant that they will not forget (as their progenitors did).

Joel 2:28–32. The Lord will pour out His Spirit upon all flesh, and the result will be prophecy, dreams, and visions. The Lord will show wonders in heaven and in the earth (blood, fire, and pillars of smoke). Before the great and terrible day of the Lord, the sun will be darkened and the moon will turn to blood. There will be deliverance in Mount Zion and in Jerusalem for those who call upon the Lord.

Malachi 3:1–4. The Lord will come suddenly to His temple. Who can abide the day of His coming? Who can stand when He appears? He is like a refiner's fire. The temple priests will be purified and officiate in righteousness as in former years.

Malachi 4:1–6. The day is coming when the proud and the wicked will be burned as with the heat of an oven. They will be burned as stubble is, so completely that nothing will be left of them (neither root nor branch). Those people who fear the name of the Lord will not be burned but will tread the ashes of the "wicked" under their feet. Elijah will be sent before the great and dreadful day of the Lord with a mission centered on turning the hearts of the fathers and their children toward each other. Accomplishment of this mission will stave off a curse with which the Lord will otherwise smite the earth.

Acts 3:22–23 [Deuteronomy 18:18–19]. Destruction is decreed for people who will not hear a prophet whom God will send unto them.

Romans 11:25. "Blindness in part is happened to Israel, until the fulness of the Gentiles be come in."

1 Corinthians 1:27–29. God has chosen the foolish things of the world to confound the wise; the weak things of the world to confound the mighty; the base and despised things of the world to bring things which are to naught.

One scripture not included in Oliver Cowdery's article or Joseph Smith's history is listed by Wilford Woodruff as being among those cited to Joseph by the angel Moroni.[3] It is **Daniel 2:44:** "And in the days of these kings shall the God of heaven set up a kingdom, which shall never be destroyed: and the kingdom shall not be left to other people, but it shall break in pieces and consume all these kingdoms, and it shall stand forever." Apparently, this scripture was not noted by Joseph Smith or Oliver Cowdery because Moroni may not have quoted it until later interviews. In commenting about his yearly visits with the angel (1824–1827), the Prophet said, "I went at the end of each year, and at each time I found the same messenger there and received instruction and intelligence from him at each of our interviews respecting what the Lord was going to do, and how and in what manner His kingdom was to be conducted in the last days."[4]

Notes to Appendix 1

1. Joseph Smith's published account of the angel Moroni's visit can be found in the *T&S,* vol. 3, no. 12, 15 Apr. 1842, 753–54. The angel Moroni made several clarifications and modifications regarding the scriptures he quoted. For instance, he said that Elijah would somehow "reveal" the priesthood, that it would be individual entities who would burn the wicked on the great and terrible day of the Lord, and that the prophet of Acts 3:22–23 was Jesus Christ (ibid.).

2. Oliver Cowdery's article can be found in two parts in *MA,* vol. 1, Feb. 1835 and Oct. 1835.

3. President Wilford Woodruff reports: "When the angel of God delivered this message to Joseph Smith he told him the heavens were full of judgments; that the Lord Almighty had set His hand to establish the kingdom that Daniel saw and prophesied about, as recorded in the second chapter of Daniel; and that the gospel had to be preached to all nations under heaven as a witness to them before the end should come, and that, too, in fulfillment of the revelation of God, as given here in the Old and New Testaments" (*JD,* 24:241).

4. *T&S,* vol. 3, no. 13, 2 May 1842, 771; emphasis added.

APPENDIX 2

THE PATTERN IN HELAMAN 14

When Helaman 14 is compared with various other canonical writings of a prophetic nature, an interesting pattern emerges. The Book of Mormon text relates that Samuel the Lamanite—at the behest of an angel of God—prophesied thousands of years ago of a series of events and messages that would occur in connection with the coming of the Son of Man. Interestingly, these same signs and messages are to be shown forth and declared as part of the grand scenario of the last days. Bruce R. McConkie notes that "it is no surprise to spiritually literate souls to learn that the prophecies of the first coming are but types and shadows of similar revelations relative to the second coming."[1] The fifteen parallels summarized in this appendix can serve a three-fold purpose: First, they can show that the events of the last days are not haphazard. God's house is a house of order (see D&C 132:8); He works according to a carefully thought-out and concisely executed plan. Second, they can act as a large-scale witness of Divine identity, demonstrating that the Messiah who will stand on the Mount of Olives is the same personage who claimed the Holy Messiahship in the meridian of time. Third, they can provide a sense of being grounded during what will surely be a period of great upheaval and uncertainty. (It is always beneficial to have an idea of what to expect in the future.)

Parallel 1

Helaman 14:2. The Son of God will come to redeem believers on His name.

D&C 43:29. "In mine own due time will I come upon the earth . . . and my people shall be redeemed and shall reign with me on earth."

Parallel 2

Helaman 14:3–4. There will be a "sign" of "great lights in heaven," insomuch that "in the night" there will be "no darkness."

Zechariah 14:4, 7. "And His feet shall stand in that day upon the mount of Olives . . . and the mount of Olives shall cleave in the midst thereof. . . . [And] it shall come to pass, that at evening time it shall be light."

Parallel 3

Helaman 14:5. A "new star" will arise as a "sign."

D&C 88:93. "And immediately there shall appear a great sign in heaven, and all people shall see it together."

Parallel 4

Helaman 14:6. There will be "many signs and wonders in heaven."

D&C 45:39–40. "And it shall come to pass that he that feareth me shall be looking forth for the great day of the Lord to come, even for the signs of the coming of the Son of Man. And they shall see signs and wonders, for they shall be shown forth in the heavens above, and in the earth beneath."

Parallel 5

Helaman 14:9. The cry is to go forth among the people: "Repent and prepare the way of the Lord."

D&C 43:20. "Lift up your voices and spare not. Call upon the nations to repent, both old and young, both bond and free, saying: Prepare yourselves for the great day of the Lord."

Parallel 6

Helaman 14:11. The "judgments" of God await those who commit iniquities.

Moses 7:66. The prophet Enoch saw, before the Second Coming, "men's hearts failing them, looking forth with fear for the judgments of the Almighty God, which should come upon the wicked."

Parallel 7

Helaman 14:15, 25. Christ will "bring to pass the resurrection of the dead."

D&C 45:46. "The Saints shall come forth [in the resurrection] from the four quarters of the earth."

Parallel 8

Helaman 14:18. The unrepentant will be "hewn down and cast into the fire."

D&C 63:53–54. "In the day of the coming of the Son of Man . . . will [the Lord] send [His] angels to pluck out the wicked and cast them into unquenchable fire."

Parallel 9

Helaman 14:20, 27. The sun, moon, and stars will be darkened as a "sign."

D&C 34:9. "Before that great day shall come [i.e., the Second Coming], the sun shall be darkened, and the moon be turned into blood; and the stars shall refuse their shining."

Parallel 10

Helaman 14:21. "There shall be thunderings and lightnings."

D&C 43:21–22. "The day cometh when the thunders shall utter their voices from the ends of the earth . . . [and] the lightnings shall streak forth from the east unto the west."

Parallel 11

Helaman 14:21. "The earth shall shake and tremble."

D&C 45:33. "And there shall be earthquakes also in divers places."

Parallel 12

Helaman 14:23. "There shall be great tempests."

D&C 88:90. There "also cometh . . . the voice of tempests."

Parallel 13

Helaman 14:23. "There shall be many mountains laid low, like unto a valley, and there shall be many places which are now called valleys which shall become mountains."

D&C 49:23. The Saints should be "looking forth . . . for the valleys to be exalted, and for the mountains to be made low."

Parallel 14

Helaman 14:24. "Many cities shall become desolate."

Revelation 16:19. A time has been foreseen when "the cities of the nations [shall] f[a]ll."

Parallel 15

Helaman 14:28–29. "Many shall see greater things than these."

D&C 29:14. "And there shall be greater signs in heaven above and in the earth beneath."

Notes to Appendix 2

1. Bruce R. McConkie, *The Promised Messiah* (Salt Lake City: Deseret Book, 1978), 31.

APPENDIX 3

An Old Testament Perspective

It is of utmost importance that the scriptures be interpreted in their proper context, and none more so than those that deal with the signs of the times, the Second Coming, and the Millennium. This appendix is offered as a tool to assist the reader in seeing pertinent scriptures from the Old Testament from a broad perspective. Hopefully, this will contribute to an accurate understanding of what the Lord has said about the prophecies of the last days in other scriptural texts.

The following storylines or patterns are substantially the same as those in the Apostle John's book of Revelation. The Lord always tells a consistent story about the signs of the times, the Second Coming, and the Millennium, but He often does not relay that story in its fullness; sometimes He even seems to combine various elements in a somewhat shortened version. This can lead to confusion if a student of the scriptures sees only a few scattered elements of the story in a text and tries to draw conclusions from that single source. Learning these patterns—and then recognizing them when they appear in the Book of Mormon, the Doctrine and Covenants, and the Pearl of Great Price—will bring the reward of enlightenment.

In the information presented below, note that the oft-quoted "blood, and fire, and pillars of smoke" prophecy from Joel 2 can be properly understood by recognizing the very same pattern in Isaiah 34.

The information in each of the following sections has been arranged and summarized so that it will be easier for the reader to see the overarching themes and patterns.

The Isaiah Pattern
(34:1–10)

The indignation and fury of the Lord is upon the armies of all the nations.

The Lord will utterly destroy them.

The sword of the Lord will come down upon Idumea in judgment.

There will be a great slaughter in the land of Idumea.

The land will be soaked in blood.

The land will become "burning pitch"; the streams will be turned into pitch or asphalt; the ground will become brimstone or sulphur. This will not be quenched day or night. The smoke of it will ascend forever.

This is the day of the Lord's vengeance, recompense for the controversy of Zion.

The carcasses of the slain will stink upon the mountains.

The heavens will be rolled together as a scroll.

The stars will fall like figs from a tree.

The Ezekiel Pattern
(38:1–23; 39:1–29)

The Lord is against the great army of Gog/Magog.

This army will consist of those nations that surround Israel on all sides.

"In the latter days" it will come against Israel.

It will arise like a storm cloud.

It will have the evil intent of taking a spoil and turning its hand against the people.

The Lord allows the army to attack Israel for a purpose—to magnify and sanctify Himself in the eyes of many nations.

The Lord will become furious when the army comes against Israel.

"There shall be a great shaking in the land of Israel" so that the fish, birds, beasts, and humans will shake at the Lord's presence, the mountains will be broken into pieces (Heb. *harac*—to pull down or in pieces, break, destroy), and every wall will fall (cf. Hag. 2:6–7).

The Lord will call for a sword against Gog/Magog and "every man's sword shall be against his brother."

The Lord will "plead against" (Heb. *shaphat*—judge, pronounce sentence upon) Gog/Magog with pestilence and bloodshed and will send an overflowing rain of great hailstones, fire, and brimstone.

The army will be turned back; only a sixth part will be left.

The Lord will give the dead bodies of the army to the ravenous birds and the beasts to be devoured. The Lord will invite the animals to this feast.

The Lord will send fire on Magog.

The weapons of war will be burned for seven years.

The dead will be buried for seven months.

The bodies of the army of Gog/Magog will stink.

The Lord will pour His Spirit upon the house of Israel and not hide His face from them anymore.

Israel will know from that day forward that Jehovah is their God.

The Joel Pattern
(2:1–11; 3:1–19)

Blow the trumpet in Zion; the day of the Lord is nigh at hand; who can abide the great and terrible day of the Lord?

It is a day of clouds and thick darkness.

Men of war in battle array; great and strong; the appearance of horsemen. There has never before been the like. Fire devours before them and flames burn behind them; they make noise like fire that devours stubble; they desolate the land.

"The earth shall quake before them; the heavens shall tremble: the sun and the moon shall be dark, and the stars shall withdraw their shining."

The Lord will direct His great army.

The Lord says, "I will show wonders in the heavens and in the earth, blood, and fire, and pillars of smoke. The sun shall be turned into darkness, and the moon into blood, before the great and the terrible day of the Lord come . . . The sun and the moon shall be darkened, and the stars shall withdraw their shining."

There will be deliverance in Mount Zion and in Jerusalem for those who call upon the Lord.

In those days the Lord will gather all nations to the valley of Jehoshaphat (Armageddon) and will judge and pass sentence on them for scattering Israel and dividing His land. "I return your recompense upon your own head," declares the Lord.

There will be "war"; there will be multitudes in the valley of decision.

Edom and Egypt will be desolate.

Their wickedness is great.

The Lord will utter His voice from Zion and Jerusalem "and the heavens and the earth shall shake."

A "fountain" will come from the house of the Lord.

The Zechariah Pattern
(12:2–11; 13:1–9; 14:1–21)

The day of the Lord cometh.

All the people of the earth will be gathered against Judah and Jerusalem and will siege them.

The city of Jerusalem will be taken; half of the city will go into captivity.

The Lord will fight against those nations that battle against Jerusalem; the Lord will smite the enemy and their horses; the Lord will defend the inhabitants of Jerusalem and destroy "all the nations" that come against Jerusalem.

The Lord and the Saints will stand on the Mount of Olives; the mountain will cleave in two and a great valley will be formed; the inhabitants of Jerusalem will flee through the valley.

From Geba to Rimmon (south of Jerusalem), all the land will be turned into a plain and lifted up.

There will be no night.

Fire will devour the enemy.

The Lord will smite those who fight against Jerusalem with a plague: "Their flesh shall consume away while they stand upon their feet, and their eyes shall consume away in their holes [Heb. *chowr*—sockets], and their tongue shall consume away in their mouth."

The Lord will cause a great tumult (Heb. *m^{e}humah*—confusion, uproar) to come upon them. "And they shall lay hold every one on the hand of his neighbor, and his hand shall rise up against the hand of his neighbor." The animals of the enemy will be plagued.

There will be mourning in "the valley of Megiddon."

Two-thirds will die; one-third will remain and be tried and refined. The Lord says, "They shall call on my name, and I will hear them: I will say, It is my people: and they shall say, The Lord is my God."

The inhabitants of Jerusalem will look upon the Lord whom they have pierced; they will mourn for the Firstborn Son. Someone will ask Him, "What are these wounds in thine hands?" Then He will answer, "Those with which I was wounded in the house of my friends."

There will be a "fountain" opened for sin and uncleanness; living waters will go out from Jerusalem.

The Lord will be King over all the earth.

APPENDIX 4

NOTES ON REVELATION 5–21

The book of Revelation can be a perplexing and daunting text to comprehend, yet the Prophet Joseph Smith declared it to be "one of the plainest books God ever caused to be written."[1] This appendix provides insights from the Prophet on the content of this apocalyptic document, as well as a synopsis of the chapters in the book of Revelation that are related to the signs of the times, the Second Coming, and the Millennium.

Doctrine and Covenants 77 contains a series of questions and answers about the book of Revelation. The answers provided by the Prophet Joseph Smith offer the following insights:

Some of the imagery in the book of Revelation should be understood in figurative terms (see v. 2, 4).

The book with seven seals mentioned in Revelation 5 contains "the revealed will, mysteries, and the works of God; the hidden things of His economy concerning this earth during the seven thousand years of its continuance, or its temporal existence" (v. 6). "The first seal contains the things of the first thousand years, and the second also of the second thousand years, and so on until the seventh" (v. 7).

The four angels mentioned in chapter 7, verse 1, are "sent forth from God," and they are "given power over the four parts of the earth, to save life and to destroy; these are they who have the everlasting gospel to commit to every nation, kindred, tongue, and people; having power to shut up the heavens, to seal up unto [eternal] life, or to cast down to the regions of darkness" (v. 8).

"The angel ascending from the east [in chapter 7, verse 2] is he to whom is given the seal of the living God over the twelve tribes of Israel; wherefore, he crieth unto the four angels having the everlasting gospel, saying: Hurt not the earth, neither the sea, nor the trees, till we have sealed the servants of our God in their foreheads. And, if you will receive it, this is Elias which was to come to gather together the tribes of Israel and restore all things" (v. 9).

The sealing of the servants of God is to take place after the sixth seal of the book is opened (see v. 10). The 144,000 persons who are sealed out of the tribes of Israel "are high priests, ordained unto the holy order of God, to administer the everlasting gospel; for they are they who are ordained out of every nation, kindred, tongue, and people, by the angels to whom is given power over the nations of the earth, to bring as many as will come to the church of the Firstborn" (v. 11).

"In the beginning of the seventh thousand years will the Lord God sanctify the earth, and complete the salvation of man, and judge all things, and shall redeem all things, except that which He hath not put into His power, when He shall have sealed all things, unto the end of all things; and the sounding of the trumpets of the seven angels [in chapter eight of the book of Revelation] are the preparing and finishing of His work, in the beginning of the seventh thousand years—the preparing of the way before the time of His coming" (v. 12).

The little book eaten by John in Revelation 10 is symbolic of a mission to be accomplished by the Apostle John in connection with the gathering of the tribes of Israel. "This is Elias, who, as it is written [in JST, Matt. 17:9–14], must come and restore all things" (v. 14). "According to John Whitmer's *History of the Church* (ch. 5): [In June 1831], 'the Spirit of the Lord fell upon Joseph [Smith] in an unusual manner, and he prophesied that John the Revelator was then among the Ten Tribes of Israel who had been led away by

Shalmaneser, king of Assyria, to prepare them for their return from their long dispersion, to again possess the land of their fathers.'"[2] In Joseph Smith's theology, the name "Elias" stood for the "office and calling" of a person who was to "prepare the way for [something] greater." "That person who holds the keys of Elias [has] a preparatory work."[3]

The two witnesses in Revelation 11 "are two prophets that are to be raised up to the Jewish nation in the last days, at the time of the restoration, and [these witnesses are] to prophesy to the Jews after they are gathered and have built the city of Jerusalem in the land of their fathers" (D&C 77:15).

The following synopses of relevant chapters in the book of Revelation are presented to help the reader more easily compare the imagery and message of this collection of texts with those that are presented in Appendix 3 of this book and in the Book of Mormon.

Chapter 5

God the Father (enthroned) holds in His right hand a book with seven seals (see v. 1).

A strong (Greek: *ischuros*—mighty, valiant) angel asks the question, "Who is worthy to open the book?" (v. 2).

No man in heaven, on earth, or under the earth is worthy to perform the task (see v. 3).

John weeps much because nobody can open, look upon, or read the book (see v. 4).

One of the elders tells John not to weep, because Jesus Christ is worthy to read the book (see v. 5).

Jesus Christ approaches the throne of the Father and takes the book (see v. 6–7).

The four beasts and twenty-four elders sing of Christ's worthiness (see v. 9–10).

These individuals are joined by many thousands of angels in proclaiming Christ's worthiness (see v. 11–12).

Every creature in heaven, on earth, under the earth, and in the sea gives praise to the Father and the Son (see v. 13).

The four beasts say, "Amen" (this is one of the titles of Jesus Christ; see Rev. 3:14); the twenty-four elders fall down and worship (v. 14).

Chapter 6

The Son of God opens the first seal; thunder is heard. The first of the four beasts tells John the Revelator, "Come and see" (v. 1).

John sees a man with a bow on a white horse. The man is given a crown and goes forth conquering (see v. 2).

The second seal is opened; the second of the four beasts says, "Come and see" (v. 3).

A man on a red horse is given a great sword. This man is given power to take peace from the earth—the inhabitants will kill one another (see v. 4).

The third seal is opened; the third of the four beasts says, "Come and see" (v. 5).

A man on a black horse has a pair of balances in his hand (see v. 5).

A voice amidst the four beasts says, "A measure of wheat for a penny, and three measures of barley for a penny; and see thou hurt not the oil and the wine" (v. 6).

The fourth seal is opened; the fourth of the four beasts says, "Come and see" (v. 7).

A man named "Death" sits on a pale horse; "Hell" accompanies him. Power is given to them over a fourth part of the earth to kill with sword, hunger, death, and beasts (v. 8).

The fifth seal is opened; martyrs appear under the altar (of incense in the heavenly temple, because they are about to pray) and ask the Lord how long it will be until He avenges their blood with judgment on the earth. They are given white robes and told to rest for a little season until others are killed like unto them (see v. 9–11).

The sixth seal is opened; there is a great earthquake, the sun is blackened, the moon appears as blood, stars fall to the earth (see v. 12–13).

The "heaven" (Greek: *ouranos*—sky) is rolled together like a scroll; every mountain and island is moved (Greek: *kineo*—stirred) out of their places (v. 14).

The men of the earth (of all classes) hide themselves in dens (Greek: *spelaion*—caverns) and among the rocks of the mountains (cf. Isa. 2:19). They call upon the mountains and the rocks to fall upon them so as to hide them from the face of the Father and the wrath of the Son: "For the great day of His wrath is come; and who shall be able to stand?" (v. 15–17).

Chapter 7

John sees four angels stand on the four corners of the earth and withhold the wind so that it does not blow on the earth, sea, or trees (see v. 1). (These angels are given power to hurt these elements of creation [see v. 2].)

John sees another angel with the seal of God ascend in the east (see v. 2).

This angel tells the four angels not to hurt the earth, sea, or trees until the servants of God are sealed in their foreheads (see v. 3).

From each of the twelve tribes of Israel, 12,000 people are sealed—making a total of 144,000 individuals in all (see v. 4–8).

John sees an innumerable host from all nations, kindreds, tongues, and peoples standing before the throne of God and the Son of God; they are clothed with white robes and hold palms in their hands. They cry out in praise of the salvation given through the Father and Son (see v. 9–10).

All the angels, the twenty-four elders, and the four beasts fall down before the throne and worship God (see v. 11–12).

One of the twenty-four elders asks John about the identity and origin of the people in white robes. John is told that they came out of great tribulation and have washed their robes white in the blood of the Lamb, i.e., have been forgiven of sin through the Atonement (see v. 13–14).

John is told that because of the condition of the people in white robes they can serve God in His heavenly temple. They do not hunger, thirst, or suffer from the heat of the day because the Father and the Lamb provide them with food and drink and wipe away all their tears (see v. 16–17).

Chapter 8

The seventh seal is opened; there is silence in heaven for about half an hour (see v. 1).

John sees seven angels stand before God; they are each given a trumpet (see v. 2).

Another angel, with a golden censer, stands at the golden altar (of incense before God's throne); he is given much incense to offer with the prayers of all the Saints (see v. 3).

The incense smoke and prayers of the Saints ascend before God—out of the angel's hand (see v. 4).

The angel fills his censer with coals/fire from the altar and casts the contents to the earth; there are voices (Greek: *phone*—noises, sounds), thunders, lightnings, and an earthquake (see v. 5).

The seven angels with trumpets prepare to sound their instruments (see v. 6).

The first angel sounds; hail and fire mixed with blood are cast upon the earth; one-third of the trees are burned and all of the green grass is burned (see v. 7).

The second angel sounds; a great mountain burning with fire is cast into the sea; one-third of the sea becomes blood, one-third of the sea creatures die, and one-third of the ships at sea are destroyed (see v. 8–9).

The third angel sounds; a great star from heaven named Wormwood, burning like a lamp, falls upon the third part of the rivers and also upon the fountains of waters; one-third of all water becomes bitter; many men who drink the water die (see v. 10–11).

The fourth angel sounds; one-third of the sun is smitten, one-third of the moon is smitten, one-third of the stars are smitten; all of them are "darkened." "And the day shone not for a third part of it, and the night likewise" (v. 12).

John sees an angel flying through the midst of heaven and hears him say, "Woe, woe, woe, to the inhabiters of the earth by reason of the other voices of the trumpet of the three angels, which are yet to sound!" (v. 13).

Chapter 9

The fifth angel sounds (first "woe" or exclamation of grief); a star from heaven falls to the earth. The star is given the key of the bottomless pit; the star opens the bottomless pit; smoke—like from a great furnace—arises out of the bottomless pit. The smoke darkens the air and the sun (see v. 1–2).

Locusts come out of the smoke and go upon the earth. The locusts are given power like scorpions. They are commanded to hurt men who do not have the seal of God in their foreheads but are commanded not to hurt trees, grass, or any green thing (see v. 3–4).

The locusts do not have power to kill men but only to hurt them as scorpions would. They are limited to torment men for five months (see v. 5).

Men will desire death because of this torment but they will not die (see v. 6).

The angel of the bottomless pit (Hebrew—*Abaddon,* Greek—*Apollyon*) is the king over the locusts. The locusts have faces like men, hair like women, teeth like lions, tails like scorpions, breastplates like iron, crowns like gold, are shaped like battle horses, and sound like battle chariots (see v. 7–11).

The sixth angel sounds (second "woe"); a voice from the four horns of the golden incense altar in the heavenly temple tells the sixth angel with the trumpet, "Loose the four angels which are bound in the great river Euphrates." The four angels are loosed; they, in conjunction with an enormous army of otherworldly beings, slay the third part of men with plagues—but even then the remainder will not repent of great wickedness (v. 13–21).

Chapter 11

During the second "woe," two prophets in Jerusalem seal the heavens against rain, turn waters to blood, and smite the earth with plagues at their will. The beast kills them; they are resurrected after three and a half days and ascend—the same hour there is a great earthquake that destroys a tenth part of Jerusalem and kills seven thousand people.

Chapter 14

The Lamb stands on Mount Zion with 144,000 people who have the Father's name in their foreheads.

An angel is seen flying through the midst of heaven.

Chapter 15

John sees "another sign in heaven" which is "great and marvelous." It consists of seven angels (clothed in pure white linen with golden sashes) who have the seven last plagues of the wrath of God. One of the four beasts gives each of the seven angels a golden vial (Greek: *phiale*—a broad, shallow cup) that is filled with God's wrath and then the angels come out of the heavenly temple (v. 1, 6–7).

Chapter 16

A voice from the temple tells the seven angels to pour out the vials of the wrath of God upon the earth (see v. 1).

The first vial is poured upon the earth; it produces a grievous sore upon those who worship the image of the beast and have his mark (see v. 2).

The second vial is poured upon the sea; the water becomes as blood and everything in the water dies (see v. 3).

The third vial is poured out upon the rivers and fountains of waters; they become blood (see v. 4).

The angel of the waters proclaims that God's judgment is righteous since men have shed the blood of the Saints and the prophets and they are now given blood to drink (see v. 5–6).

The fourth vial is poured out upon the sun; men are scorched with fire; there is great heat (see v. 8–9).

The fifth vial is poured out on the seat of the beast; there is darkness in the beast's kingdom; those who are in the beast's kingdom receive pain (Greek: *ponos*—anguish) and sores (Greek: *helkos*—ulcers) (see v. 10–11).

The sixth vial is poured out on the great river Euphrates; the water is dried up (see v. 12).

Three unclean spirits like frogs (miracle-working devils) come out of the mouth of the dragon, the beast, and the false prophet. They are the agencies who gather the kings of the earth to "the battle of that great day of God Almighty" (v. 13–14).

The Son of God states in relation to His Second Coming: "Behold, I come as a thief. Blessed is he that watcheth" (v. 15).

The kings of the earth are gathered to a place called Armageddon (see v. 16).

The seventh vial is poured into the air; there is thunder, lightning, a plague of great hail, and the mightiest earthquake in earth's history. Babylon receives the fierceness of God's wrath; cities of the nations fall; Jerusalem is divided into three sections; islands vanish and mountains are not found (see v. 17–21).

Chapters 17–18

The judgment and fall of the Whore/Babylon the Great.

Chapter 19

John sees the heavens open and Jesus Christ, in red clothing, riding a white horse. The Lord wears many crowns; His eyes are a flame of fire. The armies of heaven (clothed in white linen) follow Christ on white horses (see v. 11–15).

An angel commands the birds to gather for the supper of the

great God (see v. 17–18).

The beast and the armies of the kings of the earth gather to make war with Christ and His army. Christ slays them with the sword of His mouth. The birds feast. The beast and the false prophet are cast into a lake of fire and brimstone (see v. 19–21).

Chapter 20

A judgment takes place; resurrection; the faithful reign with Christ for years (see v. 4–6).

An angel binds Satan with a chain for one thousand years. Satan is sealed in the bottomless pit (see v. 1–3).

After one thousand years Satan will be loosed out of his prison for a little season (see v. 3, 7).

Satan goes about to deceive the nations Gog and Magog to gather them for battle. They compass the Saints, but fire from God descends and devours them (see v. 8–9).

Satan is cast into the lake of fire and brimstone with the beast and the false prophet (see v. 10).

The Final Judgment takes place (see v. 12–13).

Chapter 21

A new heaven and new earth are created (see v. 1).

Notes to Appendix 4

1. Alma P. Burton, comp., *Discourses of the Prophet Joseph Smith* (Salt Lake City: Deseret Book, 1977), 248.
2. *HC* 1:176, note 2; emphasis added.
3. *WJS,* 327–28; emphasis added.

APPENDIX 5

PLAGUES PAST AND FUTURE

This appendix includes two sections. The first contains a recital of a Jewish view of the plagues that God brought against the nation of Egypt during the time of the prophet Moses. It provides enlightenment as to why the Lord acted in such a manner against a wicked nation. The second part of this appendix shows parallels between the plagues that were brought against Egypt and those slated to be released against the wicked world of the last days. This chart shows that the Lord will repeat His great miracles of the past, on a much larger scale, in order to once again bring about His purposes on the earth.

> God divided the ten punishments decreed for Egypt into four parts, three of the plagues He committed to Aaron, three to Moses, one to the two brothers together, and three He reserved for Himself. Aaron was charged with those that proceeded from the earth and the water, the elements that are composed of more or less solid parts, from which are fashioned all the corporeal, distinctive entities, while the three entrusted to Moses were those that proceeded from the air and the fire, the elements that are most prolific of life.
>
> The Lord is a man of war [see Ex. 15:3], and as a king of flesh and blood devises various stratagems

against his enemy, so God attacked the Egyptians in various ways. He brought ten plagues down upon them. When a province rises up in rebellion, its sovereign lord first sends his army against it, to surround it and cut off the water supply. If the people are contrite, well and good; if not, he brings noise makers into the field against them. If the people are contrite, well and good; if not, he orders darts to be discharged against them. If the people are contrite, well and good; if not, he orders his legions to assault them. If the people are contrite, well and good; if not, he causes bloodshed and carnage among them. If the people are contrite, well and good; if not, he directs a stream of hot naphtha upon them. If the people are contrite, well and good; if not, he hurls projectiles at them from his ballistae. If the people are contrite, well and good; if not, he has scaling-ladders set up against their walls. If the people are contrite, well and good; if not, he casts them into dungeons. If the people are contrite, well and good; if not, he slays their magnates.

Thus did God proceed against the Egyptians. First He cut off their water supply by turning their rivers into blood. They refused to let the Israelites go, and He sent the noisy, croaking frogs into their entrails. They refused to let the Israelites go, and He brought lice against them, which pierced their flesh like darts. They refused to let the Israelites go, and He sent barbarian legions against them, mixed hordes of wild beasts. They refused to let the Israelites go, and He brought slaughter upon them, a very grievous pestilence. They refused to let the Israelites go, and He poured out naphtha over them, burning blains. They refused to let the Israelites go,

> and He caused His projectiles, the hail, to descend upon them. They refused to let the Israelites go, and He placed scaling-ladders against the wall for the locusts, which climbed them like men of war. They refused to let the Israelites go, and He cast them into dungeon darkness. They refused to let the Israelites go, and He slew their magnates, their first-born sons.[1]

The Egyptian Plagues and the Book of Revelation Signs

Below, in the set of Egyptian judgments, four instances of pestilence are manifest. However, in the corresponding last-days judgments, only two of these are matched, and they are pestilences of evil spirits. Pestilences of the ordinary kind, however, have been foretold in the Joseph Smith Translation of Matthew 24:30.

River turned to blood; fish die, water stinks and is undrinkable (Ex. 7:16–25).
Water becomes blood and everything in it dies (Rev. 16:3–4).

Frogs (Ex. 8:1–15).
Frogs/evil spirits (Rev. 16:13).

Lice/gnats (Ex. 8:16–19).
No corresponding pestilence.

Flies (Ex. 8:20–32).
No corresponding pestilence.

Disease and death of cattle (Ex. 9:1–7).
Food supply of cattle and other animals is destroyed (Rev. 8:7).
Boils on animals and people (Ex. 9:8–12).

Grievous sore appears on people (Rev. 16:2).

Hail, fire, and thunder (Ex. 9:13–34).
Hail, fire, and thunder (Rev. 16:8, 18, 21).

Locusts (Ex. 10:1–20).
Locusts/evil spirits (Rev. 9:3–4).

Darkness (Ex. 10:21–29).
Darkness in kingdom of the beast (Rev. 16:10).

Death of people (Ex. 11:4–5; 12:29–30).
Third part of men killed (Rev. 9:18).

Red Sea dries up; becomes path to complete destruction (Ex. 14:21–30).

Euphrates River dries up; it is prepared as the "way of the kings of the east" who will perish at Armageddon (Rev. 16:12).

Notes to Appendix 5

1. Louis Ginzberg, *The Legends of the Jews* (Philadelphia: The Jewish Publication Society of America, 1983), 2:341–43.

SELECTED BIBLIOGRAPHY

BOOKS

Bott, Randy L. *Home with Honor* (Salt Lake City: Deseret Book), 1995.

Brewster Jr., Hoyt W. *Doctrine and Covenants Encyclopedia* (Salt Lake City: Bookcraft), 1988.

Brown, Matthew B., and Paul Thomas Smith. *Symbols in Stone: Symbolism on the Early Temples of the Restoration* (American Fork, UT: Covenant), 1997.

———. *The Gate of Heaven: Insights on the Doctrines and Symbols of the Temple* (American Fork, UT: Covenant), 1999.

Burton, Alma P., comp., *Discourses of the Prophet Joseph Smith* (Salt Lake City: Deseret Book), 1977.

Clark, James R., comp., *Messages of the First Presidency of The Church of Jesus Christ of Latter-day Saints,* 6 vols. (Salt Lake City: Bookcraft), 1965–1975.

Cowley, Matthias F. *Cowley's Talks on Doctrine* (Chattanooga, TN: Benjamin E. Rich), 1902.

———. comp., *Wilford Woodruff: History of His Life and Labors* (Salt Lake City: Deseret News Press), 1916.

Dahl, Larry E., and Donald Q. Cannon, ed., *Encyclopedia of Joseph Smith's Teachings* (Salt Lake City: Bookcraft), 1997.

Draper, Richard D. *Opening the Seven Seals: The Visions of John the Revelator* (Salt Lake City: Deseret Book), 1991.

Durham, G. Homer, ed., *The Discourses of Wilford Woodruff* (Salt Lake City: Bookcraft), 1969.

Ehat, Andrew F., and Lydon W. Cook, ed., *The Words of Joseph Smith: The Contemporary Accounts of the Nauvoo Discourses of the Prophet Joseph* (Provo, UT: BYU Religious Studies Center), 1980.

Esshom, Frank. *Pioneers and Prominent Men of Utah* (Salt Lake City: Utah Pioneers Book Publishing Co.), 1913.

Faulring, Scott H., ed., *An American Prophet's Record: The Diaries and Journals of Joseph Smith* (Salt Lake City: Smith Research Associates), 1987.

Ginzberg, Louis. *The Legends of the Jews,* 7 vols. (Philadelphia: Jewish Publication Society of America), 1983.

Hinckley, Gordon B. *Discourses of Gordon B. Hinckley, Volume 2: 2000–2004* (Salt Lake City: Deseret Book), 2005.

Jessee, Dean C., ed., *The Personal Writings of Joseph Smith* (Salt Lake City: Deseret Book), 1984.

Kimball, Spencer W. *Faith Precedes the Miracle* (Salt Lake City: Deseret Book), 1972.

Kohlenberger III, John R., and James A. Swanson, *The Strongest Strong's Exhaustive Concordance of the Bible* (Grand Rapids, MI: Zondervan), 2001.

Ludlow, Daniel H., ed., *Encyclopedia of Mormonism,* 4 vols. (New York: Macmillan), 1992.

Ludlow, Victor L. *Unlocking the Old Testament* (Salt Lake City: Deseret Book), 1981.

———. *Isaiah: Prophet, Seer, and Poet* (Salt Lake City: Deseret Book), 1982.

Lund, Gerald N. *Selected Writings of Gerald N. Lund: Gospel Scholars Series* (Salt Lake City: Deseret Book), 1999.

Matthews, Robert J. *Selected Writings of Robert J. Matthews* (Salt Lake City: Deseret Book), 1999.

Maxwell, Neal A. *Sermons Not Spoken* (Salt Lake City: Bookcraft), 1985.

———. *Look Back at Sodom* (Salt Lake City: Deseret Book), 1975.

McConkie, Bruce R. *Mormon Doctrine,* 2d ed. (Salt Lake City: Bookcraft), 1966.

———. *Doctrinal New Testament Commentary,* 3 vols. (Salt Lake City: Bookcraft), 1973.

———. *The Promised Messiah* (Salt Lake City: Deseret Book), 1978.

———. *The Mortal Messiah* (Salt Lake City: Deseret Book), 1979.

———. *The Millennial Messiah* (Salt Lake City: Deseret Book), 1982.

———. *A New Witness for the Articles of Faith* (Salt Lake City: Deseret Book), 1985.

McIntosh, Robert, and Susan McIntosh, ed., *The Teachings of George Albert Smith* (Salt Lake City: Bookcraft), 1996.

n. a., *Masterful Discourses and Writings of Orson Pratt* (Salt Lake City: Bookcraft), 1962.

n. a. *The Essential Joseph Smith* (Salt Lake City: Signature Books), 1995.

Palmer, Spencer J. *The Expanding Church* (Salt Lake City: Deseret Book), 1978.

Parry, Donald W., Jay A. Parry, and Tina M. Peterson, *Understanding Isaiah* (Salt Lake City: Deseret Book), 1998.

Penrose, Charles W. *Rays of Living Light from the Doctrines of Christ* (Salt Lake City: Deseret News Press), 1954.

Peterson, Mark E. *Joseph of Egypt* (Salt Lake City: Deseret Book), 1981.

Pratt, Parley P. *A Voice of Warning and Instruction to All People* (Salt Lake City: Deseret News Press), 1874.

———. *Autobiography of Parley P. Pratt,* rev. ed. (Salt Lake City: Deseret Book), 2000.

Richards, LeGrand. *Israel! Do You Know?* (Salt Lake City: Deseret Book), 1954.

Roberts, Brigham H. *New Witnesses for God,* 2 vols. (Salt Lake City: Deseret News Press), 1909.

——. *A Comprehensive History of The Church of Jesus Christ of Latter-day Saints*, 6 vols. (Salt Lake City: Deseret News Press), 1930.

——. ed., *History of the Church,* 7 vols. (Salt Lake City: Deseret Book), 1948–1950.

Rust, Richard D. *Feasting on the Word: The Literary Testimony of the Book of Mormon* (Salt Lake City and Provo, UT: Deseret Book and The Foundation for Ancient Research and Mormon Studies), 1997.

Smith III, Hyrum M., and Scott G. Kenney, comp., *From Prophet to Son: Advice of Joseph F. Smith to His Missionary Sons* (Salt Lake City: Deseret Book), 1981.

Smith, Joseph F. *Gospel Doctrine* (Salt Lake City: Deseret Book), 1986.

Smith, Joseph Fielding. *The Signs of the Times* (Independence, MO: Zion's Printing and Publishing Co.), 1943.

——. *Church History and Modern Revelation,* 4 vols. (Salt Lake City: The Church of Jesus Christ of Latter-day Saints), 1946–1949.

——. *Man: His Origin and Destiny* (Salt Lake City: Deseret Book), 1954.

——. *Doctrines of Salvation,* 3 vols. (Salt Lake City: Bookcraft), 1954–1956.

——. *Answers to Gospel Questions,* 5 vols. (Salt Lake City: Deseret Book), 1957–1966.

——. *The Way to Perfection* (Salt Lake City: Deseret Book), 1966.

Snow, Eliza R. *Biography and Family Record of Lorenzo Snow* (Salt Lake City: Deseret News Press), 1884.

Sperry, Sydney B. *The Voice of Israel's Prophets* (Salt Lake City: Deseret Book), 1952.

Stuy, Brian H., ed., *Collected Discourses,* 5 vols. (Burbank, CA: B.H.S. Publishing), 1987–1992.

Talmage, James E. *The Vitality of Mormonism* (Boston: Gorham Press), 1919.

——. *A Study of the Articles of Faith* (Salt Lake City: The Church of Jesus Christ of Latter-day Saints), 1950.

Taylor, John. *The Government of God* (Liverpool, England: S. W. Richards), 1852.

Taylor, Samuel W. and Raymond W. Taylor, *The John Taylor Papers: Records of the Last Utah Pioneer*, 2 vols. (Redwood City, CA: Taylor), 1984–85.

Turley Jr., Richard E. *Victims: The LDS Church and the Mark Hofmann Forgeries Case* (Urbana and Chicago: University of Illinois Press), 1992.

Watt, George D., ed., *Journal of Discourses,* 26 vols. (Liverpool, England: Samuel W. Richards and Sons), 1853–1886.

Webster, Noah. *An American Dictionary of the English Language* (New York: S. Converse), 1828.

Whitney, Orson F. *Life of Heber C. Kimball* (Salt Lake City: Kimball Family), 1888.

——. *Saturday Night Thoughts* (Salt Lake City: Deseret News Press), 1921.

Widtsoe, John A. *Joseph Smith—Seeker after Truth, Prophet of God* (Salt Lake City: Bookcraft), 1951.

——. *Priesthood and Church Government,* rev. ed. (Salt Lake City: Deseret Book), 1954.

Williams, Clyde J., ed., *The Teachings of Harold B. Lee* (Salt Lake City: Bookcraft), 1996.

——. *The Teachings of Howard W. Hunter* (Salt Lake City: Bookcraft), 1997.

ARTICLES

Browning, Paul K. "Gathering Scattered Israel: Then and Now," *Ensign,* July 1998, 54–61.

Holland, Jeffrey R. "Terror, Triumph, and a Wedding Feast," *Brigham Young University 2004–2005 Speeches* (Provo, UT:

Brigham Young University, 2005), 3.

Jackson, Kent P. "The Appearance of Moroni to Joseph Smith," in Robert L. Millet and Kent P. Jackson, ed., *Studies in Scripture, Volume 2: The Pearl of Great Price* (Salt Lake City: Randall Book, 1985), 336–63.

——. "Moroni's Message to Joseph Smith," *Ensign,* Aug. 1990, 12–16.

——."God's Work in the Last Days," in Kent P. Jackson, *From Apostasy to Restoration* (Salt Lake City: Deseret Book, 1996), 100–14.

——. "The Latter-day David," in Kent P. Jackson, *Lost Tribes and Last Days* (Salt Lake City: Deseret Book, 2005), 107–11.

Nibley, Preston. "What of Joseph Smith's Prophecy That the Constitution Would Hang by a Thread?" *Church News,* 15 Dec. 1948, 24.

Nyman, Monte S. "When Will Zion be Redeemed?" in Leon R. Hartshorn, Dennis A. Wright, and Craig J. Ostler, ed., *The Doctrine and Covenants: A Book of Answers* (Salt Lake City: Deseret Book, 1996), 137–55.

Ostler, Craig J. "Isaiah's Voice on the Promised Millennium," in *Voices of Old Testament Prophets* (Salt Lake City: Deseret Book, 1997), 61–85.

Pixton, Paul B. "'Play it Again Sam': The Remarkable 'Prophecy' of Samuel Lutz, Alias Christophilus Gratianus, Reconsidered," *Brigham Young University Studies,* vol. 25, no. 3, Summer 1985, 27–46.

Stewart, Michael D. "What do we know about the purported statement of Joseph Smith that the Constitution would hang by a thread and that the Elders would save it?" *Ensign,* June 1976, 64–65.

Taylor, J. Lewis. "How shall I read the parables of preparation in Matthew 25 in the context of the last days?" *Ensign,* June 1975, 22–23.

Turner, Rodney. "The Two Davids," in Richard D. Draper, ed., *A*

Witness of Jesus Christ (Salt Lake City: Deseret Book, 1990), 240–57.

Wells, Rulon S. "A Fraudulent Prophecy Exposed," *Improvement Era,* vol. 11, no. 3, Jan. 1908, 161–64.

INDEX